# NEVER BEEN HEXED

### WITCHING HOUR BOOK 2

### CHRISTINE ZANE THOMAS

Copyright © 2020 by Christine Zane Thomas

All rights reserved.

No part of this book may be reproduced in any form or by any electronic or mechanical means, including information storage and retrieval systems, without written permission from the author, except for the use of brief quotations in a book review.

Cover designed by William Tyler Davis using Deposit Photos stock.

❀ Created with Vellum

# NEVER BEEN HEXED

CHRISTINE ZANE THOMAS

WITCHING HOUR

1

## GHOST DAD

Even in the midst of a crisis, sleep is a necessity.
Sleep called to me. It begged.
I said no.

The problem was after going several nights with little to no sleep, staying up all hours poring over spell books and researching, I was no closer to an answer than when I'd started this whole endeavor.

My life is just one gigantic crisis. It doesn't help that I've just turned forty.

And no, I didn't go out and buy a new Corvette. My crisis started with something crazier: me becoming a witch. But it didn't come with the elation of getting a Hogwarts' letter. It came with a raccoon familiar named Brad and an overbearing grandmother whose magical teaching style was to give me just enough rope—and by rope, I mean magic—to spell myself off a tree on Gallows Hill.

Even now, with Brad gone, Gran did little to help get him back. It was me who did the heavy lifting—the reading, skimming over spell after spell in hopes of finding the right one. But every time I found something, anything I thought might be worthwhile, it usually left me with more questions than answers. These questions spun in my head every night, so even when I did try to sleep, it almost never found me.

I wasn't trying to sleep.

No, I was hoping not to. With a book at my desk, right next to Gran's old Singer, and my bed a few feet away, I studied until exhaustion got the better of me. The letters began to bend and morph. I read them over and over again, not making heads or tails of their meaning.

Unlike eating—or other forms of self-care—a body can force sleep. No matter how much caffeine in my bloodstream, no matter how determined I was to struggle through one more page, my body was done. Reluctantly, I gave in.

I turned off my lamp and crashed into bed, snuggling under the too warm comforter and allowed sleep to wash over me like a wave.

"Constance." My father's voice mingled with the dream I was having.

Maybe it wasn't a dream but a memory. My mother's blue eyes peered down at a younger, smaller version of me. Current me, at nearly six-feet tall, wouldn't need to crane my neck to see into those eyes. They were so light. I could almost see through her. My mother's eyes really were windows into her soul—a soul that went missing shortly before I'd turned ten years old, over thirty years ago now.

"Constance," my father said again, distant—like maybe he was in the next room. Like he was calling to me in the memory. I fought the urge to leave my mother's side. I wanted to stay. I wanted to be with her, if only for a little while longer. My father could wait.

"Constance, I need you to wake up."

Isn't that how all dreams end—with a need to wake up? It's never a want. Not really.

My eyes fluttered open. They struggled, squinting against a pale luminescence in the room. It was still dark outside, but the room was oddly bright.

My body protested, having not had nearly enough sleep. I ached in several places. My back. My knees. My hips. My mind was much the same, not yet engaged with the guilt it had been feeling over the past few weeks—the guilt from losing Brad. It was the reason I couldn't sleep and why my bouts of insomnia were at an all-time high.

*Curse this crisis.*

"Five more minutes," I said out loud and closed my eyes once more.

"Constance." My dad's voice again.

Present.

Here.

Here in this room.

I jerked up, fully awake, threw the bedsheet off, and scrambled for my laptop. I thought I must've left it open. Usually, we FaceTime called or used Skype every few days. I didn't remember him telling me he was going to call tonight. But he must have.

I squeezed my burning eyes closed against the wisp of pale energy in the room, not yet registering what it was. Not until *it* said my name again. The ghost of my father.

Henry Campbell, age sixty-eight, should've been at his home outside San Diego, California. Like me, he should've been asleep in his bed. Instead, he stood at the edge of mine, looking oddly like water vapor—a fuzzily outlined bright blue mist.

He wasn't wearing any clothes below the neck, but his body was just a man shape. No muscles, no skeletal structure. No other appendages. He was a blur. His hands and feet were barely realized. When he moved, they stayed a moment like tendrils of water vapor, of mist, slowly catching up with the rest of him.

In life, my father had grown old. His hair was gray, almost white. He wore glasses. His eyes had been a brownish gray. And he sported a full beard. I couldn't recall the last time I'd seen his upper lip.

This face was nothing like that. It was more like the man I remembered from my childhood, from around the time of that memory of my mother. *Was it a dream or a memory?* I wondered. Sometimes it's both.

*And is this a dream?*

I would've screamed, had I not been dumbstruck. The hairs all over my body were standing on end. Then I realized that the hairs all over my body were in plain sight. In my sleep, I'd taken off my nightshirt. July had made the second story of my Gran's house, where I slept in her spare bedroom, sweltering hot.

I stood frozen in the middle of the room, laptop in hand, wide-eyed in just light pink panties.

The specter of my father winced. "You don't wear PJs anymore, sweetheart?"

"Uh..."

The comforter, which I'd half-kicked to the floor, dangled at the edge of the bed. I wrapped it around my shoulders like a shawl.

This had to be another dream. One of those *Inception* deals. But regardless, I had to take precautions.

"Dad?" I asked. It's hard to know what you'd say or do when confronted by a real ghost—not until it happens. This seemed like a bad start.

"It's me, sweetie."

"Dad, you're a—"

"A ghost. I know."

I pinched my forearm. It didn't hurt. I decided I hadn't pinched hard enough. The next time, I meant it. And the next time, I felt it. Pain throbbed from the spot.

Still, I wasn't convinced.

I read somewhere that one way to tell if you're dreaming is to find a clock. My phone would have to do. Except I couldn't remember what to do when I looked at the clock. It looked normal. It looked like several hours before sunrise.

"You're not dreaming," the ghost of my father said.

"That sounds like something someone would say in a dream," I replied.

"You're right. It does, doesn't it?" He kind of smiled. "Tell you what. I'll prove it. Ask me something only I would know. Ask me anything."

I shook my head. "That doesn't really work either. If I ask you something, you'll either know it because you know it or because—"

"Because you know." He nodded, his face blurring up and down. "Because it's your consciousness. Yeah, I get it. But maybe it doesn't matter if you think you're dreaming or not. Either way tomorrow comes—and with it the news."

"What news?"

"The news of my death," he said.

Stinging tears filled my eyes, streaming down my cheeks. At that moment, I knew I wasn't dreaming. Those were real tears.

"You can't be dead."

"But I am."

"How? And how are you a ghost?"

In any normal circumstance, I'd probably be questioning this whole scenario—I'd think it was some joke. But the crisis—the crises.

My life had taken several twisting turns since learning

that I was a witch—from a long line of witches, including my grandmother and my mother. I'd found out that my mother, who I thought died in a plane crash, might not be so dead after all. She'd gone missing after starting a job for a mysterious paranormal organization known as the Faction.

Then, before I could even come into my powers, I stumbled across the body of my former boss, only to find out he was a vampire. I got dragged into his murder investigation by the local sheriff, a werewolf. A ruggedly handsome werewolf.

In the end, I'd almost been killed for those magical powers. And Brad had been taken. He was trapped somewhere in the shadow realm.

So, a ghost in my bedroom hardly seemed out of the norm. Just another night in this midlife curse.

I shuddered as new anxiety mixed with the old. My father was gone. And he was a ghost.

"That's why I came here," he said. "They're going to tell you I died of natural causes. Who knows—a heart attack or something like that."

"Okay."

"But it's not true. I don't know how I died, Constance. I heard voices. Unnatural voices."

"Whose?"

"I don't know who." His voice was so distant, an echo of what I was used to hearing. Even that started to fade. "Honey, there's something I've been meaning to talk to you about."

I nodded encouragingly. I wanted him to spit it out. Whatever he wanted to say, we were going to figure this out... together. All of it—who killed him and how.

I had the urge to run to Gran, to see if there was any way

of changing him back, although I'd seen *Practical Magic* enough times to know that probably wasn't a good idea.

"Your mom," he began, "she told me something once." His body started fading. He whispered and it barely reached my ears. "She told me she was a witch."

"I'm one too."

"She was working for someone. Working on something. Trying to find something."

"Dad."

He waved his phantom arm from in front of his face. "This form doesn't want to stay here long."

"What do you need to tell me?" I pressed.

"I think… I think maybe I was killed by magic."

It made no sense. There was no way he could know that. And yet…

"I have to go," he said.

"Don't," I pleaded. "We can fix this. You just have to stay here. I'll go get Gran." If anyone would know how to fix this, it'd be my eighty-something-year-old grandmother.

"I'll try to come back," Dad said.

"You will?"

"I'll try my best."

"No. What does that even mean?"

He smiled, still fading away. "It means I'll try my best."

"No, Dad," I argued. "It means you're not going to. You've been saying 'I'll try my best' my whole life—your whole life—and its definition is 'it probably won't happen.' I need you to promise me."

It wasn't that Dad wasn't reliable. He was almost too reliable. Always there. Always willing to help. But I'd heard this particular phrase often enough to know its meaning well. His way of saying something isn't a good idea. And he's often right.

"What do you want me to say, Constance? I don't know what's across that plane. But I do know I want to go there. And I can't stay here."

"It's not what I want you to say. It's what I want you to do. I want you to come back. We have to finish this conversation. I need to know more about Mom—about what happened to you."

"I'll try my best," he said again.

Then the bright glow dwindled to a dimming ball at the center of his chest. Then the ghostly form of my father winked out of existence. Possibly for good.

## 2

## IN WITCH WE TALK MAGICAL MURDER

There was no getting back to sleep. Not after that. My circadian rhythm was probably permanently damaged anyway—out of sync like a middle school marching band.

I felt clammy and cold. With my breathing shallow and my heart racing, I realized I was probably in shock. I sprawled out on the bed and tried to get it together.

With a little focus, my magic found its way to me, manifesting with a slight burning in my fingertips. Sometimes, I had to find it. I had to dig deep into the well of magic that lived inside me. Other times, it found me—because when it thought I was too stupid to go on living, it had to make a course correction.

Weirdly, the news of my father's death didn't hit me with the sort of sucker punch it would have had I gotten a phone call or heard it from the local authorities—from my friend the local sheriff, Dave Marsters, a werewolf. I found some comfort in hearing it from the man himself. His spirit.

Some comfort. Not a lot.

My father had been murdered. Or at least he thought so.

We had no proof, and neither would the police—not if he was killed by magic.

*But how? Is it even possible?*

I considered that. *Almost anything is, it being magic and all.*

I was tempted to run to Gran's room, burst through her door, and explain everything. Gran was my mother's mother, and I'd only recently moved in with her. Just before my fortieth birthday—when my whole world came crashing down. Before that, we'd been estranged for most of my life. So, she'd never been the first person I went to with my problems. That person had been my dad. He could solve anything from a scrape on a knee to a divorce from a cheating husband.

Gran, on the other hand, had a limited set of skills. Hers revolved around magic. And this was a magical problem after all. With her help, and with some from my paranormal friends, we were sure to figure this thing out.

I decided to wait for sunrise. Gran wouldn't appreciate being woken up. Not again—for the umpteenth time in the past few weeks. I'd made the mistake of trying to enlist her aid in retrieving Brad, banished from the world into the shadow realm by the same evil warlock who'd tried to take my powers.

Familiars are fallen angels. They aren't demons like you might think—they're actually neutrals in Heaven's war with Hell, a war that still rages to this day. Once fallen, they come to Earth and are paired with witches and a few other paranormal entities, protecting them from the evils within the shadow realm. Usually. Unless they get stuck in it themselves. This had been Brad's first time as a witch's familiar. And he was off to the worst of starts.

So, that's what I'd been doing—searching for a way to get him back.

Unfortunately, there's no witchy dark web. My online searches about magic only pulled up joke results. But my friend Trish owned a used bookstore that specialized in magic and the occult. I worked there a few days a week, manning the storefront and shipping orders to witches around the world.

In the weeks since Brad's disappearance, I'd spent most of my spare time combing the shelves for anything that might help us in our search. Only now, that search had to go to the back burner. My dad came first. I'd spent the last forty years with him, and only about a month with Brad.

And I still wasn't clear on a familiar's importance. It was like being given your mother's pearl necklace as a little kid and losing it playing dress up, only to figure out on your wedding day why it was important.

I waited for the sun to shine through the narrow slit in the curtains. I waited. And I waited. And...

"Constance." Gran shook me awake. "Your boyfriend's here. And he says it's urgent."

I blinked. *Did I fall asleep?*

"He's not my boyfriend." But I knew exactly who Gran was talking about. Dave was downstairs, here to deliver news I already knew.

My heart sank. I hadn't even had time to pretend it was a dream.

While I'd meant to stay awake, it was better that I hadn't. My body felt rested. I took a deep breath. It was filled with the scent of morning—one nice surprise about being a witch was how connected to nature, to Mother Earth, I felt. I smelled foggy moisture and the sweetness of grass clippings. I caught the drone of one of the neighbors mowing his grass.

"Put on a shirt," Gran spat. "And a bra, if you don't want

your moneymakers to show." She looked me over. "I don't know, maybe you do. Yes, best you go without."

"I don't want my moneymakers to show," I told her. "And they have not, nor will they ever make any money."

"Suit yourself. I think you've still got a few years left before..." She held her palms up in front of her then dropped them to her belt. "And I was going to say they *might* go lopsided, then I noticed that right one. She doesn't want to look me in the eye, if you know what I mean."

"Gran!" I shook my head. "Get out. I'll be down in a minute."

She didn't leave. She studied my face intently and said, "What's wrong?"

"This isn't good news," I said.

"Ah, so you know what he's here about, do you? That bugger wouldn't tell me. I guess I should've known it wasn't good." Gran stayed in the doorway. "Well?"

"I'll explain everything when I get down there."

I found my bra and snapped it on, then pulled my shirt over my head. I wasn't ready for Dave to see that side of me, despite what I'd seen of him. We'd had one date. It didn't go well. It started out okay, we'd gone to the town's Midsummer Festival with his three girls—Dave is a widower. Then the full moon happened. Only, there wasn't supposed to be a full moon that night. Dave and most of the other shifters in town turned. I'd seen him in his wolf form. And while he wasn't threatening to me in any way, it still scared the life out of me.

I put on a pair of old running shorts and looked myself over in the bathroom mirror. My eyes were puffy, my cheeks too. My blonde hair was a rat's nest.

*If you can't love me at my worst*, I thought, then plodded down the stairs.

Dave was seated at Gran's kitchen table. He was in his uniform, all browns and khaki, a ball cap with the sheriff's department badge on his head. Like me, he was taller than average. Over six feet, he had long limbs, strapped with lean muscles. Dave's dark eyes wouldn't meet mine.

Something about him had changed, and it took me a second to figure out what it was. Then it hit me—the thick mustache that adorned Dave's wide lips was gone, replaced by the same stubble as the rest of his face. He'd shaved it—possibly for me. I'd only suggested it half a dozen times.

"I like it." Those were the first words out of my mouth.

He looked confused. "You like what?"

I reached out to stroke his face. He recoiled, then recovered, swiping at his lip with his own thumb. "Right," he sighed. "I, uh, sorry. I forgot I did this. I look eighteen again."

"You looked like this when you were eighteen?"

His head pitched downward. "Well, I was a bit leaner."

"What's the werewolf doing here?" A cat leaped onto the kitchen table. Stevie had the appearance of a black Maine Coon with a graying mane. He was Gran's familiar. A familiar's appearance is a construct of his witch's choosing. Once a familiar and a witch make their bond, their familiar's form sets until they meet the next witch and the cycle begins anew. His throaty voice—like the sound of scraping metal—could only be heard by witches.

Dave's ears, which I imagined were sharpened by being part wolf, were lucky to only hear the purr of a cat.

Gran shuffled in a moment later, a cup of coffee in hand. The words encircling the mug read *Spelling Up Trouble*. Words she took a little too literally.

"All right." she said. "Are you ready to tell us what this is about?"

"I, uh..." Dave still avoided my eyes, looking everywhere but at me. He was struggling.

"It's all right," I said. "I know."

"You know what?" Gran groused.

"That my dad died last night."

"He what?" She spit out her coffee.

And I hurried to get Dave and myself a cup of coffee.

Dave took his cup and finally met my eyes. He looked relieved.

"I wasn't sure how to tell you," he said frankly. "Sometimes we get these calls—they're favors, really. They didn't want to call you so late last night. When they told me who it was, well, I volunteered."

"But how do *you* know?" Gran asked. "Have you all of a sudden developed a third eye?"

"I don't think it works like that," Dave offered.

His deputy, Willow, practiced in the psychic arts. Or the psychic arts practiced on her. Her foresight was never in response to her own will. She couldn't force it. And her visions often came at inopportune times—like when she was trying to capture a bad guy. When a vision happened, it made her stop in her tracks, supplanting her view of the real world for that of the future.

Gran harrumphed. "You will not come to my house and talk about magic like you know an ounce about it, David Marsters."

"Duly noted, ma'am."

"Now, please, Constance. Sit down. Drink your coffee. And tell us how you know about your father's death."

I sat. I explained how his ghost had appeared and everything we'd talked about before he vanished.

"That's good," Gran finally said.

"What is?"

Stevie, who'd been listening patiently on the table hopped down and stalked out of the room with his tail raised.

"I believe he's heard enough to be dangerous," Gran said, then she turned to me. "I meant that it's good that he chose to go and didn't try to stick it out as a ghost."

"Why?"

"Because ghosts have a half-life in every sense of that word. His spirit would fade... eventually. But well before then, all of your father's memories, every vestige of his being would leave. He'd become a haunt to whoever came near him and wherever he stayed. Trust me. It's for the best if you don't see him again in this world."

"But he told me he'd be back."

"He told you what you wanted to hear," Gran said firmly.

I hated knowing that she was right. His words repeated in my mind: "I'll try my best."

"What made him say it was magic?" Dave circled back. "Have you told him about this—about you?"

I shook my head. Then Gran gave me a hard look.

"No, I swear. He said it was Mom. I don't think he believed her at first but—"

"But now it suddenly makes sense." Gran scowled. "Men. They'll do whatever they can not to believe in life. But being a ghost puts things into a whole new perspective. It opens up certain ways of thinking."

Gran was never good at holding back. I imagined she once had a similar conversation with my grandfather. This was probably before he caught her mid-spell and had a heart attack and died—something my mother had always blamed her for.

"I still don't understand why he thinks it was magic," Gran said.

Dave chimed in, "The preliminary from the San Diego County Sheriff's office was no foul play. Most likely it was natural causes."

"Did he ingest any potions recently?" Gran disregarded Dave.

"I, uh, I didn't ask. How would he know if it was a potion and not poison?"

"They taste and feel different." Dave knew a little about potions from his last case. He'd taken one called Daylight, meant to prevent werewolves from changing into their wolf form during the full moon. It came with nasty side effects. And it turned out to be lethal to vampires. Go figure.

"You can't mask the taste of a potion—not like you can poison. Anything sweet ruins its effect. Anything else, well, let's just say, it might not be pretty."

"What do you mean you can feel it?" I asked.

"You know how alcohol burns going down?" Dave pretended to take a shot. "Well, with a potion you feel every element as it goes down your throat."

I wasn't following.

"Earth, wind, water—obviously—and fire," Gran listed them off. "You'll have to take one to know what we mean."

"Okay," I said slowly.

I crossed potions off my list of things I liked about being a witch. And that list was small. It included things like flying a broom, which I wasn't allowed to do (according to Gran), and, well, I guess that was it.

Magic is fickle. It only works if you have a real need. So trivial things like cleaning the house were mostly off the table. Why it agreed with the dark arts—why every villain had an easier go of it—was beyond me. How anyone could have a need to kill my father made no sense whatsoever.

"Listen," I said. "I don't think Dad took any potions. I think he would've mentioned it."

"Well, what *did* he mention?" Gran asked.

I thought back. I'd been so tired, so sad, and so emotional. *Why did he think it was magic?*

"He said something about voices. That's right. He said he heard voices."

"Voices?" Gran asked. "Or a voice?"

I shrugged. "I think he said voices."

Gran scowled. "That's odd."

"Isn't there some way we can ask him?" Now that Gran had put it in my mind that he wasn't coming back, I thought there must be other ways of communicating with the dead. A séance, a Ouija board.

"Like?" Gran asked.

"You know..." I already felt stupid. "A séance?"

Gran scowled. "That makes the second person at this table to talk out of turn about magic they don't understand. Mediums are rare birds indeed and most make their living talking to ghosts in the room, not crossing the plane."

"Okay," Dave said. "So, any ideas?"

She put up a finger. "Let an old woman think."

Gran closed her eyes and sat back in her chair. I went to get another cup of coffee, and she thrust her cup out, her eyes still closed, indicating she was also in need of a refill.

I was smart enough not to say a word, allowing her to think.

"I think I have it," she said.

I returned to my seat with both cups. "All right?"

"There are several curses that a witch may use to kill a person. They each have their pros and cons. Most are difficult. And almost all require something—usually blood—

from the target. Do you know if your father had any spillage of blood recently?"

"No, I don't think—" I went cold, thinking back to our last FaceTime call. "He did. I forgot. He had a physical last week. He had a neon green bandage on his arm where they took his blood. They said he was in perfect health."

"Perfect my rosy red rear end," Gran muttered.

"So, someone took his blood," Dave said. "And they used it to spell him to death? Do you think they were in the room with him?"

"Probably not," Gran answered. "Of the curses I know that require blood, the easiest to perform can be done a world away from the target. They just need the blood. But this curse allows the target to hear it when it's being cast, giving the victim a chance to counter."

"Which is fine and dandy if you're another witch," Dave started.

"But not so good if you're a regular mortal like my father," I finished.

## 3
## IN WITCH I RETURN TO CALIFORNIA

Dave gave me a few numbers to call in San Diego. And those led to others. I was overwhelmed immediately—how someone grieving is supposed to manage a funeral and an estate is beyond me. And I had to do it with thousands of miles and three time zones between us.

My Aunt Helen, who was nearly ten years younger than Dad and a realtor, offered to help. Besides me, she and her two sons, my cousins J.B. and Gage, were his only living relatives. They lived in Oregon. We saw them every few years when I was growing up. A pang of guilt hit me when I couldn't remember the last time we'd seen each other face to face. It might've been my high school graduation.

*Awkward.*

Over the phone, we opted for a small service, inviting Dad's former colleagues and his friends. I had to be on a flight to San Diego the next morning. And as far as everyone else was concerned—including the San Diego County Sheriff's Department—his death was caused by heart attack.

Only I knew different.

I still had to prove to Gran and everyone in my inner circle, Dave and Trish and the coven, that his death was magical foul play. Gran gave me a few spells and charms to snuff out any traces in his house. There was no guarantee any of them would work. And I couldn't convince her to get on the plane with me.

"I don't care about statistics," she said. "Or how reliable you say they are. I am not, nor will I ever set foot on a contraption that flies through the air by itself."

"As opposed to?"

"As opposed to one that uses magic." Gran gestured toward the broom leaning on the wall in the laundry room. "At least I know how that works."

"Except you don't," I argued. She wasn't in the mood for a fight about the workings of magic. And to be honest, I wasn't either. Except now, after what happened to my dad, I was eager to figure out this thing that had killed him. Without her, I would be left to my own witchy devices, which were lacking.

Proving magic was involved in his death was one thing, but there were a host of other issues—like, what if the killer was still around? And why? And, who were they really after? Was his death a way to get to me? To Gran?

I squirmed at the thought. All signs pointed to me. A witch's powers are most susceptible to being stolen in the first year. There are ways of extracting the power. Of taking it. Maybe someone wanted my power and they were willing to go through my father to get it.

Stevie slinked into the room while I was packing and lounged in my suitcase—in the way. Sometimes, his catlike demeanor overshadowed his wisdom. If it weren't for him talking, I'd almost believe he was an ordinary cat. Most of the time, he was a jerk anyway. Like a cat.

"Where've you been?" I asked him.

"I thought that was obvious." He licked a paw. "I was in the shadow realm ensuring your father didn't get caught there along the way."

"You were? Did you find him?"

"No."

"Wait." I turned skeptical. "Why would he be in the shadow realm?"

My understanding was that the shadow realm was where everything bad lived, everything magical and devious out to hurt witches. Those entities were why familiars were here in the first place—to protect us.

The thing about being magically trained at forty—it comes through a firehose and it's nothing like seven years of schooling at Hogwarts. Every time I thought I had a handle on it, a new factoid turned it on its head.

"The shadow realm is just a euphemism for the other side," Stevie said. "It's a construct—kind of like the way your physicists refer to the multiverse. It's a place where everything else goes."

"Like souls?"

"Like souls," Stevie acknowledged. "And demons and monsters and Fae and everything else."

"Everything's there in one place?"

"Don't think of it as *one* place. It's not. It's like an onion. Layers and layers, all of which house unique worlds. Infinite worlds. And there's not just one world for spirits. Millions, maybe billions. But the fallen aren't really welcomed in most."

"Well, that's not very convenient," I said. "Do you really think he won't come back?"

Cats can't frown, not unless they're perpetually grumpy

like that Grumpy Cat, but Stevie is different. He frowned. "It's unlikely after crossing over."

"Can I ask why you were worried? Is it just about his murder? Do you think something would've tried to harm his soul as well?"

"It's not only that," Stevie said. "I was hoping to catch him. I wanted to ask about your mother. Dying lifts certain enchantments. It opens the mind. We, that is your grandmother and I, believe that it's possible he knows more about her disappearance than he's said."

"I think he might," I agreed.

I never pressed him very hard on that subject, not even after I became a witch. Not even after I'd learned the truth about my mother. And not when he was a ghost in my room.

"What about Brad?" I asked Stevie. "Any luck there?"

Stevie had been on the hunt for Brad in the shadow realm as well. Now I understood why it was so hard. He was searching layer after layer of that infinite onion. A familiar in a haystack.

"Brad will be fine," he said.

"How do you know that?"

"Because I've lived since the dawn of time—just as he has. These years on Earth have felt like a blink of the eye. And in the shadow realm, time is different. It ebbs and flows. Wherever he is, we'll find him and set him free."

I didn't have as much confidence.

When I'd first met my familiar, all I wanted was for him not to be a rodent or a cat. I kind of hoped for a dog. But he'd latched onto a memory of Rocket Raccoon in my head and became a trash panda, complete with bandit eyes and the *cutest* whiskers. He was also a lot nicer than Stevie.

Stevie snoozed in my open suitcase while I picked out a

black dress and wrapped my head around the fact that my father was gone forever.

The next day, I put on a brave face and made the trek to the Charlottesville-Albemarle airport. Several stops later, last minute flights being what they are, I stepped out of the rental car facilities into the mild heat and California sunshine.

I knew the drive like the back of my hand.

The silence in my father's house—my home for twenty years, through high school and part of college—was deafening. It felt so much the same and yet so different. He'd remodeled the kitchen and hall bathroom almost ten years ago. But my room and my bathroom were the way I'd left them when I'd lived there. Posters hung with pink thumbtacks served as proof my mid-Nineties grudge phase had morphed into something more sinister—boy bands. I couldn't believe Dad never took them down. He never tried to make my room into a guest room. He liked to tell me that I was his only guest, and that was obviously how I wanted the room to be.

It was true, I'd visited often. But not so much after marrying my now ex-husband Mark. It wasn't so much the distance, though driving from San Francisco to San Diego was a trek, it was the disconnection. I'd allowed work and my not-so-requited love for Mark to put a wedge between us.

Guilt flooded through me, making it hard to move through the house. I should've been here. If I wasn't in Virginia learning magic this never would have happened—it was magic, and someone connected to it, that caused his death.

I could have simply renounced my powers.

Yet here I was, about to use them.

Dad's room was clean and rather sparse. There was a bed and a nightstand. A flat screen TV mounted on the wall above his dresser. Three paperback books on the nightstand, all in various stages of completion. Dad was the type to leave the book face down on his page—this was despite the many bookmarks I'd gifted him over the years or the Kindle reader I bought him that he just "couldn't figure out." His words.

Whoever had moved his body had also taken the comforter. Otherwise, the room was intact.

I stood in the middle of it, just as I'd seen Trish do when she used a summoning charm after Mr. Caulfield's death. I reached out, channeling my will from the center of my body through my index finger and out to the world at large. I chanted the words that Gran taught me, the rhyme best suited to trace magic left by the spell Gran suspected had been used to murder my father.

> "A spell was cast upon this place.
> And every spell leaves a trace.
> This is a spell with no reverse.
> Be it hex or charm or curse.
> A spell was cast upon this place.
> Send it now, give me the trace."

With my eyes closed, I waited for the wind to whisper in my ear as it had the last time I used a summoning spell.

I waited a beat longer, my ears pricked and ready. The air conditioner hummed to life. Dad always kept the house cold.

Frustrated, I opened my eyes, fully expecting to see the house as it had been the moment before. I was mistaken. The air above my dad's bed shimmered with purple sparkles of light. Tiny particles of energy zipped away, shooting through the wall toward the backyard.

I followed them outside—through the French doors, not the wall.

The wisps of purple energy ghosted through the wall—bad choice of words—and they traveled upward through the air, where they met the contrails of passing jets.

I had to see where they went.

Dad kept his broom in the hall closet. I tried to charm the thing to fly. It didn't budge. Not surprising. Magic was connected with the Earth, and this broom was as unnatural as they come, plastic handle and all. Even its bristles were nylon. There wasn't an ounce of wood or natural material in it.

I sighed.

There was no way I could follow the purple particle trail on foot. It stretched for miles, and it was still going as far as my eyes could see.

Even in my rental car, it was fruitless. I followed it for hours, twisting down roads, and eventually onto the interstate. The sun went down. The purple trace became a faint aurora in the night sky.

Eventually, I had to turn back. When I did, a spark flew from my fingertips. My fight or flight response. My magic bubbling up. But I knew one thing was certain. Magic had been the cause of his death. And I was going to find who cast that spell, and they were going to pay for what they'd done.

But I had other, more pressing things to do. More pressing even than finding my father's killer.

I had to say goodbye.

4
---

## THE MAGICAL TRACE

Four days later, I returned to Virginia with an urn and a promise from my aunt to get Dad's house sold. I'd been given a small inheritance and the promise of some insurance money. That combined with my savings meant I could do whatever I wanted for a few years. I could go anywhere. I could really start fresh.

Only I wasn't ready to leave Creel Creek just yet.

Nestled in the foothills of the Blue Ridge Mountains, Creel Creek was just a speck on the map. But unlike most, it was home to uncanny secrets. The town's current inhabitants included witches, werewolves like the sheriff and his sister, Imogene, and many other forms of shifter. And up until recently, a vampire. Mr. Caulfield had owned the grocery store where I'd worked briefly.

I passed through the outskirts of Creel Creek trying to ignore the vineyard with its creepy Addams-esque mansion overlooking the highway from the hillside.

About a month ago, a local podcast featured the vineyard in one of its episodes. The two hosts had found a real life mummy in the cellar. Luckily, that real life mummy—

and owner of the vineyard—was able to play off their discovery as a prank.

A single stretch of highway divided Creel Creek in half. I slowed, entering the speed trap before the grocery store. But my adjusted speed was temporary.

Flying home from San Diego added a whole new level of frustration to air travel. After failing to follow the purple trail the night I got home, I saw it again. From the plane window, I'd watched the city become nothing more than an anthill below us. Then the aircraft rolled toward the east and the purple trail, faint now, became visible for a while. It mocked me, paralleling the path of the plane mere feet from my window seat. If the window had been open, I could have touched it, it was so close. But airlines frown upon that.

Somewhere near the Grand Canyon, I lost it. I'd thought for good. But there it was crossing the horizon off toward the other end of town—toward Gran's house.

I put my foot down on the pedal. Crookshanks, my nearly twenty-year-old Subaru Outback, revved, then she lurched into gear. The tires hummed on the hot asphalt. That was the only sound I heard until...

*Woop! Woop!* The familiar blip of a siren pierced the air, and my cell phone began to ring. I answered through the aftermarket Bluetooth system, having to crank the stereo volume to eleven to hear the voice on the other end.

"Just what the heck do you think you're doing?" In my rearview mirror, Dave's lips were pursed. His police SUV had no trouble tailgating me, strobing blue lights and all.

"Driving," I said.

"You might call it that. But from where I'm sitting, you're going too fast and you're a tad on the erratic side. Care to explain?"

I hunched over the steering wheel, craning my neck to

get a glimpse of where the purple wisps of magic had disappeared to over the tree line.

"I'm following a trail... of magic."

"I assume this has something to do with your father's death?"

"You are correct. It's the same one I found in his house the other night."

"And where is this trail taking us?" he asked.

"I'm not sure. It looks like maybe near Gran's."

"So, you're following it home then? Constance, do you think your Gran's in trouble?"

"I... I don't know."

The thought hadn't occurred to me. But now I considered the possibility. This trace of magic led all the way from San Diego to here in Creel Creek. Meaning that the person who'd conjured the curse lived here.

"Fenny snakes," I cursed.

"Fenny what?"

"Just Gran rubbing off on me." I sighed and pushed the thought of her being in danger away. This trace was days old. And I'd spoken to Gran when I got off the plane. She'd sounded fine, if not chipper. Then again, I'd been fooled over the phone before.

"I want to check on Gran but—" I stopped talking when I found the trace again over the tree line. We were close to Gran's subdivision, coming up on the cemetery. And now I knew exactly where the trail was taking us.

"But what?" Dave asked.

"But I want to follow the source of this magic first."

"Your Gran can wait," Dave said reassuringly. "I'm right behind you."

I turned into the cemetery, followed the dirt road all the way to the fence, and stopped Crookshanks next to the chain link. Dave's SUV shuddered to a halt behind me. Then without any fanfare, another car, a canary yellow Volkswagen Beetle, turned in. It came up the dirt road only a little slower than we had.

Dave got out of the SUV and adjusted his ball cap. "Who the heck is that?"

"Trish," I said.

He shook his head. "Ah, I remember now. I stopped her going eighty last year. Pretty sure those cars—even the newer ones like hers—don't go faster than that."

The Volkswagen careened to a stop behind Dave, and Trish popped out. Unlike almost six-foot me, Trish was short and pear-shaped. Even in the summer heat, she wore black. Black jeans, a plain black t-shirt, and old-school Doc Martins. Her hair looked like the dead of night except for a streak of purple to one side of the bangs above her vivid green eyes. Today the look was finished off by a silver necklace with a Triquetra pendant.

Lately, she'd been trying to get me to wear one—to wear anything symbolizing my rebirth as a witch. The Triquetra symbolizes the power of three or the threefold nature of the Goddess as maiden, mother, and crone.

Maybe it was just me, not feeling represented. I was missing a mother, living with a crone, and at forty, I felt much more like an old maid than I had in my youth.

I took a few steps back and got a running start at the fence. I almost got stuck. My fabric Toms weren't made for climbing, but I finally managed to get over it.

"Where the heck are you going?" Dave asked.

"The graveyard." Trish hefted herself over and followed me toward the forest.

"Hello... Ladies?" Dave pointed down. "This is a graveyard."

"That's a cemetery," Trish replied. "We're headed somewhere a little more off the beaten path."

Defeated, Dave sighed. And with minimal effort, he made it over the fence.

"Can you see it too?" I asked them.

"See what?" Trish asked.

I pointed. "The magic."

Trish shook her head.

"Then why are you here?" I asked her.

"Well, I was outside the grocery store, and I saw the world's worst police chase. I figured something must be up." She shrugged, just her shoulders, with no arms involved. "So, what's up?"

"It's the trace—the spell I performed at my dad's house. It leads all the way here."

"You're kidding," Trish and Dave said, not quite in unison.

We cut through the woods until we found the worn path between Gran's house and the graveyard, a path that I'd taken a number of times over the past few weeks.

Witching from sacred ground was a way to amplify magic ability. Others included working spells or making potions during the witching hour—from midnight to one in the morning. Combine the two, and things multiplied exponentially. Our trips out here were usually in the dead of night.

I was used to the darkness when the shadows were long and every branch looked threatening, like the claw of some demon. In the afternoon sunshine, it was the opposite. It even sounded completely different. Chirping birds rather than the ill-timed hooting of owls.

I realized that the trees weren't actually very thick; each had room to grow and stretch out its limbs. The undergrowth was held at bay, not quite obscuring the path, almost as if there'd been a controlled burn in the last few months. Or maybe it was kept that way by magic. It was probably magic.

The path led out a clearing where lush green grass carpeted a hillside crowned by the rusty iron gates of the graveyard. A lone tree at the top of the hill stood among the crooked headstones and crosses.

"Creepy," Dave said.

"You never make it this way?" Trish asked him.

"No. Never."

"Not even when you're, uh... Ahoooooooo," she howled.

Dave smirked. "Nah, I try to go up to the mountains if I can. The deer's more plentiful, and there's fresh water. Let's just say if I stick around these parts, some farmers might call the office the next day about missing cattle."

"Sounds convenient, Sheriff."

"Yeah, well, I still don't like doing the paperwork." He smiled.

I continued to the massive oak tree, following the wisp of purple particles. Under the moss-covered branches, the particles floated down and settled into the silhouette of a woman, her hand outstretched, and her features nonexistent.

"Who is it?" I asked, only just remembering that I was the only one who could see her.

"I can't see whatever you're seeing. Can you maybe elaborate?"

I told her about the purple trail that led all the way from my Dad's house in California to here, basically into Gran's backyard, in Virginia. I described the outline of the person. The faintest of traces touched the trunk in the shape of a human hand.

"It's useless," Trish said. "The silhouette, I mean. I'm guessing you see a featureless blob about yea tall." She held out a hand about six inches higher than her head.

"Why do you say it's useless?" Dave asked her. "Height and build are the cornerstones of any police search."

"You're not going to get that here," she said. "It's a soul cast. They're the same height. The same build."

I put my palm where hers was and the purple particles blew away with a sudden gust of wind. The figure too—she was gone.

"So what does all this mean?" Dave asked us.

"It means," Trish said, "that someone cast the killing spell on Constance's father from this spot."

"So, it's someone local?"

"Not necessarily." Trish shook her head. "They could've used this spot because of its connection with Constance."

"How would they know about it? Unless it's someone you're connected to?"

"I'm no expert in any of this." Trish turned to me. "But it's not like your Gran keeps herself hidden. At least, not like Nell Baker did. She's known in the area. Heck, I think she's probably known throughout the whole continent."

"Great." I sighed and remembered that a few minutes ago I'd been worried about Gran. Whoever was after my dad was probably after me or her. Or both of us—for whatever reason.

"I should get back and check on her," I told them. "I just wish there was some way to tell who *owned* that magic."

"But there is." Trish nodded. "Every practitioner has their own trace. I only wish mine was purple." She winced. "Not because of this, obviously. I think mine's the same shade of green as my eyes. And yours is blue like Anakin's lightsaber."

"How do you know that?"

"I pay attention."

*Like I don't.*

"So, that's it," Dave said. "All you have to do is find that purple magic and let me know who's responsible."

"Cause that evidence is going to hold up in court?" I asked skeptically.

"We'll worry about that when we get there." He turned and peered down the slope of the hill. "You two hear something?"

We both listened. The forest wasn't exactly silent, but I didn't hear anything out of the ordinary.

"I don't." Trish shrugged.

"Me—" I couldn't get out the word *either*. Because I heard voices. Familiar voices.

The podcasters had found us.

## 5

## IN WITCH WE WERE FOLLOWED

"Fenny snakes," I cursed.

Trish scowled. "You and your gran. That's not even a real curse. Not like—"

"Shhh!" I shushed her.

"What is that?" She turned toward the commotion outside the gate.

"Dave... by any chance did you use your police scanner?"

He put his hand on his neck and grimaced. "Yeah... I might've called it in when we got to the cemetery—ya know, just in case Willow needed to know where I was."

Trish shook her head then stomped down the hill determinedly. I didn't think she wanted either of the two women now visible through the trees to set foot on the sacred ground inside the gates. We made it outside before Summer Shields, a pointy-faced redhead, stumbled onto the path.

I didn't think Summer, a local reporter and notorious eavesdropper on the police radio frequency, was here on official TV business. Her usual shadow, a dumpy cameraman, was nowhere to be seen. Instead, another somebody crept out of the woods beside her.

Holding a phone to her lips, Jade Gerwig went wide-eyed seeing the three of us staring back at her. The former butcher and now grocery manager had muscle where the reporter was skin and bone. Like Trish, I thought she must've come straight from work because she was wearing khaki pants and a polo.

The two women straightened and brushed themselves off; Summer wore a triumphant smile on her pointy face. Unofficial, indeed. This trip fell in the realm of their extracurricular activities. Together, they hosted a podcast called *Creel Creek After Dark* where they speculated about supernatural happenings around the town. Speculated being the key word—neither of them was paranormal in any way. But while most residents of Creel Creek turned a blind eye to all the weirdness, their eyes were open and looking through a magnifying glass.

"Well, if it isn't our favorite trio," Summer said loudly—for us and their listeners.

Trish muttered something under her breath, and Jade looked quizzically down at her phone then stuffed it in her pocket.

"Although," Summer said, "I thought for sure Willow was headed this way."

"Only if she had a vision that told her to be here," Dave murmured into my ear.

"Secrets don't make friends." Jade glared at us, then she nodded toward Trish. "Trish," she acknowledged.

"Jade." Trish managed to use the same tone with her boss at the grocery, not polite but not near as snippy as Summer had been.

"Favorite trio?" Dave grinned. "Well, I was just telling Constance that y'all are my favorite duo. That episode last week about the Bigfoot, it had me captivated."

"Sasquatch," Jade corrected. "Bigfoot is an all-encompassing term. The sighting was of a Sasquatch."

"I'm sure it was." Dave winked. "Either way, it was a great episode."

"Thank you. That means a lot." Summer couldn't—or wouldn't—see through the lie. "Our fanbase has more than doubled since last year. We're actually in talks about hosting a conference sometime in the fall. So, wish us luck."

"Good luck," Dave said. "Is that what brings y'all out here on such a lovely day? More podcast research? Should I be looking out for the big guy?" Dave put his hand above his brow and faux searched the area. "No bigfoot."

Jade rolled her eyes.

"Yes, well, it *is* for the show." Summer gave him a slight smile. "You brought us here. On the call, I believe you indicated that there was some sort of magic happening. We thought we'd come see for ourselves."

"Yeah, so where is it?" Jade asked.

Dave's returned Summer's smile. "Did you say magic?"

"No. You did."

He turned his head so they couldn't see him and mouthed that he was sorry.

I averted my eyes. This was *his* mess to get us out of.

He nodded and looked thoughtful. "That radio. I think it's on its last leg. What I actually said was static. The satellite at Constance's grandmother's place, it's all sorts of messed up. We thought we'd hike up to the old radio tower and give it a look."

Summer's face fell, then she bristled. "Is that really a job for the sheriff?"

"It's a funny thing being the sheriff. This city doesn't have a big budget. Lots of odd jobs fall in my lap. And Constance is a friend. I'm just doing her a favor."

"That doesn't explain why you'd rush over here," Jade pointed out.

"Crap," Trish whispered in my direction. We were about ten feet away from them now, and the confrontation was beginning to feel like a meeting between the T-Birds and the Scorpions in *Grease*. And Trish was caught in the middle.

"Why does any man do anything?" Dave asked her, a little meta. "I came in a rush because I kind of have a thing for Ms. Campbell here. I mean, look at me. I shaved my mustache. I'm even eating my vegetables."

"I'm sure you are." Jade had no other comeback.

But Summer chose to give me stank eye. Even widowed and forty plus, with three little girls at home, Dave was one of Creel Creek's most eligible bachelors. And with his words, my stomach filled with butterflies. We'd only been on the one date. And maybe this was just his tactic to get us out of their sights. But nonetheless, I felt a flutter.

I was thankful that word hadn't gotten around about my dad's death. Not yet. Had they known that I'd come here straight from the airport—with my father's ashes still buckled in on the front seat—they'd be even more suspicious.

"Now, if you two want to carry on with your podcast," Dave said, "you're welcome to. Unfortunately, there's no magic to be had. At least not that I'm aware of. And from what we can tell, no static either. I think Miss Jezebel's just going to have to get a new provider."

Summer's face puckered. "No. You know what? I think you're hiding something from us."

"Well, the thing about opinions is everyone's got one," Trish said. "I think maybe you two have seen too many episodes of *The X-Files*."

"Well, that's where you're wrong," Summer said. "I've never seen one."

"Summer," Jade intervened, "it's not worth it."

"Really? Not one?" Dave shook his head. "It's a good show."

They disregarded him and skirted us, then went through the clearing to the graveyard.

Trish sighed as they walked up the hill.

"What?" Dave asked. "They aren't going to find anything, are they?"

"That's not what I'm worried about," Trish said.

"Then what *are* you worried about?"

"I'm worried what happens when they continue to not find anything—and we're always involved."

"I'm not sure I follow," the sheriff said.

But I understood. "She's saying they know something's up... with us."

## 6

## MAGIC AND MIRRORS

I declined both Dave's and Trish's offer to meet me at Gran's house. If she was okay, their presence would only cause alarm. And this talk, I was sure, would be a delicate one.

There was someone after us—and they were closer than we could've imagined. They'd conjured the spell that killed my dad basically in our backyard.

I found Gran in the living room in her recliner, her pink fuzzy slippers propped up, in her bathrobe and with wet hair. The sound of the loud drain in the master bath gurgling making it all the way to the living room.

"You had a tub?" I asked her. "At this time of day?"

"This may come as a shock to you, Constance Campbell, but I've lived by myself for nearly half my life. And when you're gone, I march to the beat of my own drum."

"It's more like a cowbell." I pictured Will Ferrell on SNL but in Gran's bathrobe. "And don't let me stop you," I said. "I'm just glad to see you're all right."

"Why wouldn't I be?" she snapped.

It took me a while with Gran interrupting, but I got all the way to the graveyard.

"That still doesn't explain why you were worried about me," she pointed out.

"Because whoever they are, they must be after us." I thought it was obvious. I was wrong.

"Us?" She looked dubious. "You mean you!"

"No. I meant us."

Gran jerked forward, shutting the footrest with a loud snap, and almost bounced when the old chair shot her forward. I had to catch her. She scowled. "Now, I know I've made a few enemies in my life. But none so dumb enough to start a war on my home turf. I think this is about you and you alone."

"And what makes you say that?" I asked her. "I've only been witching for what, a couple of months?"

"True. But think. What've you been doing most of this last month?" She was always answering my questions with more of her own.

"I don't know. I've been looking for Brad."

"Looking for Brad *and*..."

I slapped my hand on my forehead. She was right. She was *always* right. "And my mother," I said.

Gran pointed a gnarled finger at me before heading to the stairs. "You've asked anyone and everyone what they know about the Faction. I'm guessing the word got out."

"But what does that have to do with my dad?"

"They're sending you a message."

"To stop looking? That's kind of a loud message."

"As messages go, they usually are."

And with that cryptic statement, Gran eased up the stairs, her fuzzy slippers scuffing on the carpet. I assumed she was going to put on clothes and I didn't follow. But a few minutes later, she struggled down the stairs carrying the mirror from the hall bath. Her robe had come undone and hung open.

"Gran! What are you doing?"

"Tossing it," she said matter-of-factly. "I'll need your help with the one in the master bath. And there's this one in the hall."

"You're going to toss our mirrors? Like in the trash?"

"That's the usual way." Gran never did the *usual* way.

"Why?"

"Because they're dangerous. A mirror can be used as a window—sometimes a door. Do you want this person who's after you knowing where you are at all times? What you're doing? And do you want them in the house?"

I shook my head.

"Then grab the hall mirror," she said. "We'll put them all in the garage under a sheet for now. No need to throw them away unless..."

"Unless what?"

"Unless they've already been using one."

"You think?"

"If they already know this mirror leads into the house, then no cover on it will do. They could still use it as a door. Now, have you seen anything strange in the mirror lately?" she asked.

"Just my reflection."

No matter the amount of fiction I'd consumed in my youth, I was still learning what was real in the witching world. Using mirrors as windows and doors sounded more like something out of novel.

I took a wary look into the hall mirror. The crow's feet were more pronounced, as were the bags under my eyes.

Forty hit me harder than any other year and the year was just starting.

"Only your reflection? You're sure there wasn't anyone behind you? And were your eyes the right color?"

"Always blue."

"Good. Good." Gran nodded. "Still, best we shatter them to be sure. It'll be nice to let out some anger."

We went to the garage, our mirrors in hand, and Gran opened the garage door. The evening sun was turning orange above the mountains. Opposite, a row of purplish clouds threatened, slowly moving toward us, their color reminding me of the magic used to kill my father. It was going to storm.

Inside, I felt the rage that Gran already knew was there. She was right. I needed to let out my fury.

We edged past the covered Buick that Gran never drove. I went to her tool chest to retrieve a hammer.

"There's no need for that." Gran twirled her finger, just as she did every time she worked a spell. "We'll get out some *magical* energy while we're here."

She set the mirror down, leaned it on one of the trash cans outside, and stepped back about ten feet.

"Into a thousand pieces or more,
make certain this mirror cannot be a door.
Let no one watch us unaware
break this mirror beyond repair."

The mirror exploded into more than a thousand pieces, closer to a million. The pieces of deadly shrapnel floated in the air, just hovering, until Gran said,

"One by one and two by two,

Into the trash can, all of you."

The glass listened.

Some spells—most spells—didn't require a specific set of words. Just a rhyme that made loose sense, and more importantly, knowing what you wanted to happen. A force of will, a bit of emotion, and a few words—that was all you needed.

But there are others where no matter what words I tried, no matter how specific the thought behind them, the spell wouldn't work without the exact right words with the *exact* right emotion and will. Magic is complex like that. Then again, so is everything else. Most anyone can put together a classical physics formula but try to do some quantum mechanics and see what happens.

"Your turn." Gran took several steps farther back than I had. And as usual, she'd made the right decision. I tied far too much emotion to the original spell and was lucky not to be cut to ribbons. The explosion wrapped around me, pointed shards mere inches from my eyeballs and the rest of me.

"I knew you were upset," Gran said after I'd spelled them into the bin. "But honestly, you've got to maintain more control. Magic is a knife. Maybe a gun. It's not a stick of dynamite."

"Gran..."

"I know," she said soothingly. "I know you're hurting. I'm sorry that I was insensitive to that."

"It's not that."

"Then what is it?"

"I don't know." I struggled to place the mixed emotions, then latched on to a few. "I want to know who did this. And I want to get them back."

"We'll figure it out," she promised. "And we'll find your mother too. If only you could talk to your father one more time, then maybe—"

"That's it," I cut her off. "I have to talk to him."

She frowned. "That's impossible, dear. Once they cross over, they don't come back."

"He said he would."

"Constance, I'm no expert on the matter. The best we can do is to figure out who killed him and why. And make sure they don't do anything else."

She was right about that. "Trish said there's a way we can find out whose magic I followed today," I said. "But how? Do you think someone local is working for the Faction?"

"I know one way to find out." Her eyes narrowed. "We'll call a meeting of the local witches for the next crescent moon. And we'll test anyone who shows up."

"Right." I nodded. "*If* they show..."

"They will. Until then, we should keep the news of your father's murder to ourselves. Because they can't know—"

"That we do," I finished.

Later, the storm broke outside. I tried to fall asleep to the rain and the thunder, but I just couldn't. I kept seeing my dad in his ghost form there by the bed. Or hoping to.

Then I got a notification on my phone. A special episode of my *favorite* podcast was now available.

I pressed play.

# 7
## CREEL CREEK AFTER DARK EPISODE 53

*It's getting late.*
*Very late.*
*The creeping dread of tomorrow haunts your dreams.*
*It's dark out. Are you afraid?*
*Welcome to Creel Creek After Dark.*

**Athena:** I'm your host, Athena Hunter.

**Ivana:** And I'm Ivana Steak. We're here this week to discuss some local events.

**Athena:** Some *suspicious* local events, Ivana.

**Ivana:** We want to say thanks to everyone who wrote in, commented, and liked the Sasquatch episode last week. We promise to have updates soon on North America's most mysterious mountain dweller.

**Athena:** And like we said last episode, he's known to be lurking somewhere near the foothills of the Blue Ridge Mountains, just outside of Creel Creek, Virginia. Book your next stay at Creel Creek Mountain Lodge and receive 10% off and a free continental breakfast for using the code

PODCAST52. That's PODCAST, all upper case, and the numbers five and two.

**Ivana:** Have you ever stayed there, Athena?

**Athena:** I can't say I have, being local and all. You?

**Ivana:** Once.

**Athena:** And?

**Ivana:** And that's where I had my first paranormal sighting.

**Athena:** Not Bigfoot though, right?

**Ivana:** Sasquatch.

**Athena:** Whatever. You know what I mean. Was it the big guy?

**Ivana:** No. That night I saw a ghost.

**Athena:** Wait... how have I never heard this?

**Ivana:** I don't know. Maybe because at the time, I didn't believe it myself. I was in the middle of a breakup. I moved out. I just needed a place to crash for the night.

**Athena:** And you're sure you saw a ghost?

**Ivana:** That's kind of the thing with all of this, isn't it? I'm sure of what I saw, but no one else will be unless they see it with their own eyes.

**Athena:** Do you have any idea who you saw? What they looked like?

**Ivana:** I don't want to sound cliché. It always seems like ghosts are from long ago, sometime in the past. And this guy, I'm pretty sure he was one of the miners, the ones we've talked about on the show—from that unexplained explosion in the 1800s. But I can't tell you how I know that.

**Athena:** Why not?

**Ivana:** Because I don't know myself. It's not like he was wearing any sort of mining getup. His body looked kind of blurry. His face looked worn, almost leathery but in that same blurry way.

**Athena:** What'd he do?

**Ivana:** He just stared at me. Like the perfect amount of time. Not too long, but a stare. Then he smiled. And despite being upset about my breakup, despite seeing a ghost, I smiled back. I should've been scared, I know. But I wasn't. Nothing about it was scary. It's weird, right?

**Athena:** I don't think it's weird. You're the one who's always a bit skeptical of all this. I'm sitting here with goosebumps.

**Ivana:** Yeah, well, as I said I can't even be sure it wasn't a dream. And speaking of skeptical, we should say that we're skeptical of a few of our locals.

**Athena:** That's right. Nice segue, by the way! This week, we were casually planning this episode together when we heard the word magic on the police scanner. Not kidding. Actual, real life, magic.

**Ivana:** Only, it wasn't. Or they claim it wasn't. We've told you about these three in earlier episodes. And like we do for ourselves and our guests, we protect their real identities. On *Creel Creek After Dark*, we call them The Hound, The Bookish Witch, and The New Girl. Make sure to listen to episodes 48 and 49, or to episode 15 and 23 for a rundown on these three and the mysterious circumstances they've been involved with.

**Athena:** Then we followed them to the location of said magic where they jerked us around a bit.

**Ivana:** They were in the graveyard. Yes. *The* graveyard. You know the one. We followed them there. And they couldn't—no, they wouldn't—tell us why the call about magic went out.

**Athena:** The Hound wanted us to believe that our ears had deceived us—that he'd actually said the word static. Now, do static and magic sound similar to you?

**Ivana:** They do not, Athena. This goes back to what we were just talking about. Self-doubt. Or, even worse, the introduction of self-doubt by someone else.

**Athena:** And this is something these three do often. A month ago, at our Midsummer Festival, they did something to introduce doubt in hundreds of attendees. We just can't prove it.

**Ivana:** So, we're reaching out to our listeners. If you know something, if you've seen something—

**Athena:** Or heard it.

**Ivana:** Then please, contact the show. We'd love to have you or your story. And if you come across these three—The Hound, The Bookish Witch, and The New Girl—and they do anything suspicious, we'd love to hear about that too.

**Athena:** Until next time. This has been *Creel Creek After Dark* with your hosts Athena Hunter...

**Ivana:** And Ivana Steak.

## 8
## IN WITCH A BOOK ARRIVES

The next day, I attempted to get back some normalcy and went back to work at Bewitched Books. Trish was happy. I was able to woman the counter at her used bookstore while she went to her job at the grocery.

Across from the charred shell of the old county courthouse, Bewitched Books was one of only two open shops on Main Street.

The store housed an eclectic collection of used books which included typical genres like romance, science fiction, and mystery. Those rows of yellowing paperbacks were what one expects from a used bookshop. The other half of the store, dedicated to the sale and resale of books on the supernatural and occult, were what set the store apart.

These were books of real magic. Most had found their way to the store through a summoning spell Trish's mother had sent out to the world. When a witch or wizard died, their old books made their way here somehow.

No one came in for the first few hours. That wasn't unusual. The majority of our customers were online. I boxed and shipped several orders that Trish found the time to do while I was away.

The quiet did nothing to slow my racing mind. I didn't think removing a few mirrors was enough to ward us against something like what happened to my father.

The only company I had was Twinkie, Trish's familiar. The little mouse dozed in her drawer nook beside the register. Like Stevie, she'd been spending a fair amount of her time in the shadow realm, searching for Brad. And from what I'd gathered, the hours spent there were draining.

"Are you doing all right, little one?" I asked Twinkie when she emerged from the drawer. She stretched her tiny legs and did a few yoga poses, not unlike a cat or a dog after a long nap.

"I'm fine." Her voice, the same guttural voice of any familiar, invaded the space around me. It came from nowhere and everywhere—everywhere except her tiny mouse lips, which hadn't moved.

"I could do with some cheese though," she said, a hint of her chipper personality shining. If I had to choose between Stevie and Twinkie, I'd take the latter.

"Hmm. I think I packed a block in my lunch. Almost like I knew you might be interested."

"You know you don't have to do that," Twinkie said. "I'm happy to help look for Brad. It's just tiring."

"Why though?"

"Have you ever shifted forms? That's a piece of it. Then there's the shadow realm itself. Magic in its rawest form. Just being around it drains you."

I gave Twinkie the piece of cheese, and she nibbled on it. Eating or not, she continued talking, a reminder the form and the familiar were not a being. The mouse was just a construct.

"Do you know why it's called the shadow realm?" she asked.

"Not really." I shrugged and offered, "I've heard it's like an onion?"

"In the most basic sense, yes. In the first so-called layer, everything looks like a shadow of this one. Kind of like a black and white TV show. From there, you see the shadows of this world. But you can't interact with them, not really."

"What's the next layer?"

"That's where things get tricky," she said. "There isn't just *one*. You can't step through from one to the next and the next. The first layer is the portal to all of the others. They each have their own gates—their doors. Members only. Some have been locked away for eternities. Some have been lost."

"I thought it would be easier,"

"To find Brad or to talk to your father?" she asked knowingly.

"Either."

"Where your father is—it's a place the fallen aren't allowed."

"And where Brad is? Any ideas?"

"No good ones."

That wasn't good to hear. His banishment was my fault, just like Dad's murder was my fault.

Probably.

*I'm a witching wrecking ball.*

If I could get word to my father, talk to him one last time, ask him about my mother, I'd be content. Or I thought I'd be. I'd be one step closer to finding my mother. To find her, I'd have to go through the Faction, who were probably responsible for my dad's murder.

Brad was a whole other problem. I wanted him back,

there was no question there. I just couldn't see how it was going to happen.

The two losses felt connected in some twisted way. Like one might lead to the other.

Twinkie cast around for crumbs, then patted the slight bulge in her belly. "Thank you for the cheese."

"Thank you for the help," I said.

The mouse retreated to the back room which housed a portal to the shadow realm, only accessible to familiars. There were a few others scattered around town. I didn't know where.

I spent the next hour combing through books that Gran and Trish thought might help, but nothing popped out at me.

And no one came into the shop until right before closing when the door chimed.

I leaned over to see who'd come in. The list of contenders was especially short. Either Trish had gotten off early from work or one of the other witches about town was in need of a book. There was a slim chance that it would be Cyrus Tadros, our local mummy and owner of the vineyard and the grocery.

But the woman at the door was none of them. Granted, I didn't know every witch in the area—just the few that had been to my birthday ritual or I'd seen in the shop.

This woman looked too young. Not yet forty. Not yet a witch. She had dirty blonde hair she wore long and straight over a sunflower print sundress and a crossbody saddlebag. I wanted to ask her where she bought her flat sandals. She was long legged and pretty, and she smiled shyly at me.

"I... I'm not sure I'm in the right spot," she said meekly, venturing toward the counter past the aisles of used books.

"Are you looking for a used bookshop?" I returned her smile.

"I'm looking for someone to take this." She opened her bag to reveal an old leather-bound book. Some of its pages were loose, and they jutted out at odd angles.

"You're in luck. We buy used books." I eyed it speculatively. I'd never actually been here when a spell book arrived. I thought they came by FedEx or something, not from young women with no clue what they were holding.

"Oh... cool." She held the book close, not offering it to me. "It's just... I'm not sure why I'm here."

"You're not?"

"No." She shook her head. "Where is here?"

"This is Creel Creek. Where are you from?"

"Virginia Beach."

"That's a long drive."

She nodded.

"Can I ask how you came to have the book?"

"It's kind of a long story," she said.

I indicated the empty shop. "I think I have the time, if you do."

She laughed a little. "It's from my grandmother. She died recently."

"Oh, no! I'm so sorry—"

She shook me off. "It's okay. We weren't close. I didn't actually know her. My mom—she gave me up for adoption. My birth father's sister took me in. And they raised me as their own. When my dad died in a motorcycle accident, I still called him Uncle Randy—I didn't know he was my real dad.

"A few years later, they told me everything. And they said that my mom's mom—my grandmother—always wanted to see me. I guess my mom didn't feel the same way."

"Ouch," I said.

She shrugged. "But the timing just never worked out. I had cheer camp the summer she wanted to visit, and she didn't like phones for some reason. Old people. No offense."

I took offense.

"When I was college," the girl continued, "my grandmother offered to let me stay with her. She said she had something she wanted to tell me, but she never did. We lost touch after that. Or rather, I stopped reading her letters. It felt so old-timey. And really, I didn't feel connected to her or my mother. So, I didn't see the point."

I felt for her. Had things gone differently in my own life, I could've been in the same place. Except I had a great dad. And Gran was pretty great once I got past her Gran-isms.

"Her lawyer tracked me down last week," the woman said. "This is everything she left me. This old book. That's it. I can't even understand the pages. It's like they're written in a different language."

"Are they?"

"No. That's the weird thing. I can read the individual words, but when I put them together, they just don't make sense. Have you ever read a book like that?"

"Maybe? I think it was by Jonathan Franzen."

She chuckled.

"How old are you?" I asked her.

She took a moment. "Twenty-eight. I'll be twenty-nine in October."

She was eleven years away from coming into her powers. That was a long time for a spell book to sit idle. So, the way I understood it, it was looking for a short-term home. And it found one, thanks to Trish's mother's spell.

"Let's take a look. I'm sure I can make an offer," I told her.

"Really?" The girl held up the ragged book. "Are you sure it's worth anything?"

"I'll look it up in our database."

Trish had taught me a charm that told the true worth of a book. Though what they were wasn't often monetary. Like the worth of *War and Peace* was a door stop. And the worth of *Pride and Prejudice* was a night without sleep. But most books had a value of something or another. Every used book by Terry Pratchett was worth about five dollars.

"Do you mind if I take it?" I asked her.

She didn't actually seem like she wanted to part with it. Reluctantly, she gave me the book then smiled nervously.

"This will just take a moment." I set the book down next to the little tablet we used as a register. Trish had worked the spell to use its display. I put down the book, stared at the screen, and whispered the incantation.

After a moment, jumbled letters appeared. After moving into order, they said: *A father's words.*

I gasped. My heart began to pound in my chest. It was almost as if the book was searching me out, not the store. I knew in my bones it would have whatever I needed to communicate with my father again. I couldn't wait to pay her for it and have it to myself. I typed on the tablet, pretending to be checking for a price. I carefully inspected the cover and its pages. Finally, I was ready to make an offer.

"I can offer you fifty dollars." I held my breath.

"Fifty? Really?"

"Really."

"I didn't realize it'd be worth that much." She snatched the book up. "I wonder if I could get more somewhere else."

"There's a limited number of collectors of books like

this," I told her, which was the truth. I couldn't help that she didn't know she was a witch. "We serve a number of them online," I said.

"So, you don't think I could do better on eBay?"

I shrugged. "Probably not. Tell you what. How about a hundred dollars?" Trish only kept a hundred dollars on hand at the store. If I wanted to go higher, I'd be using my own money.

She perked up. "Thanks, but I think I'll—"

"Fine. Two hundred dollars. Final offer." It was all I had in my pocket. Another hundred I'd kept for travel emergencies when in California.

"No. I think I'll keep it. Thanks."

I realized that I'd made several missteps. And now she probably thought the real value of the book was somewhere upwards of five hundred dollars or more. When, to me, its value was priceless. And to others, probably less. I was the one who wanted the book—who needed it. No one else would see its value like I had.

"Is there anything I could do to change your mind?" I asked her.

"I don't think so."

"We could keep it for you. We could restore it, just until you find it a new owner." I was desperate.

"I really don't think so." She smiled again, but this time it was fake. She clutched the book to her chest and rushed out of the shop. The chime on the door rang twice, first when she shoved the door open wide, and next, when it bounced to a close.

"Fenny snakes," I cursed.

## 9

## WINE AND WITCHES

Later, I recounted the events to Trish, who'd come in from her shift at the grocery store with a bottle of wine, a pizza, and two pints of ice cream. We were set for another night of scouring texts looking for help to return Brad from the depths of the shadow realm, except my heart wasn't in it.

The other familiars were only so much help. While they could slip in and out of the shadow realm with ease, they had no clue what it was that kept him bound there. It had to be magic of some sort.

And despite the familiars being, pardon the pun, familiar with all things witchy, neither Stevie nor Twinkie had ever come up against anything quite like this. They'd both served a long line of witches through numerous lifetimes. Stevie had rarely heard of this sort of thing happening. And he'd never heard of one coming back.

The book with the spell that banished Brad had disappeared without a trace. Trish had tried every summoning spell she could think of to get old Nell Baker's book. But until she did, we were limited to what she had in stock.

"That's a shame," Trish said after I'd finished the story.

"What is?"

"That girl. She kept a book she won't be able to use."

I wasn't following.

Trish went to the back room and found a corkscrew. The wine was from our local Armand Vineyards, a simple red blend.

"She won't be able to use it," Trish explained. "You said the words were jumbled to her, right? And she'd lost her mom and grandmother without ever knowing they were witches?"

I nodded. "Right. So, she won't be able to use it, not until she's forty."

"Not ever." Trish held a half-eaten slice of pizza inches from her lips. "Her connection with magic is broken. You could tell her now that she comes from a long line of witches and I don't think it would matter."

"You're sure?"

"My best guess," Trish said. "I think her link is broken."

To think, if Gran hadn't lured me here to Creel Creek before my birthday, I'd be normal. No magic. And maybe none of this would've happened. My dad would still be around. I'd probably be living with him in California, and not here waiting for my aunt to sell his house. I'd be able to talk to him. To see him.

"That wouldn't have been as easy for you as you think." Trish poured me a glass of wine when she saw I hadn't.

I liked it, but thanks to a birthday gift from one of our local witches, I was impervious to most poisons, including alcohol. I couldn't get drunk. Not even tipsy.

"Why not?" I asked her. "Our stories are much the same."

"Because you had—have—a connection with your mother. And she's not dead. We know she's not."

"We don't know. Not for sure."

"You do." Trish's vivid green eyes penetrated my soul. For someone so new in my life, she sure knew me well.

"Speaking of my mom," I changed the subject on her, "what I know for sure is that my dad is dead. And I want to talk to him about her. About his death. I want to say a proper goodbye."

"You're saying you want that book."

"I already said I wanted the book. I offered her two hundred dollars."

Trish laughed. She flipped the purple lock of hair off her face and tucked it behind her ear. "Fine. Let's get you that book."

"Is it that easy?"

"I'm checking to see if she put it online." Trish typed on the screen.

"Has she?"

"Hold on. It's not like I can magic a—oh, *curses and cauldrons*, I can."

"What's that?"

"My new curse words. To match your lame 'fenny snakes.' But then again, a good F bomb works just as well."

Trish closed her eyes and whispered a spell.

We waited.

"No, it's not there." She shook her head and the purple streak flopped over her face again. "But if she does, we'll get a notification."

"Cool," I said. "So modern. I didn't think technology and spells worked together."

"They don't. This isn't a real tablet. It's a piece of wood with runes written on it. It's spelled to look this way."

Trish got two more slices of pizza, filled her glass, and wiggled the wine bottle in my direction. "You know, there might be other ways to get the information you're after."

"From Cyrus?"

Cyrus Tadros, or Osiris as he's called in legend, came to Creel Creek sometime between the late eighteenth and early nineteenth centuries. Of course, he'd been around much longer than that. After being murdered, his wife Isis, a witch like us, created wrappings with restorative properties that Cyrus used to restore himself back to youthful vigor. He'd been in the middle of his transition from elderly Edward Armand to Cyrus Tadros when the podcasters stumbled upon his sarcophagus.

Cyrus was also somewhat of a ghost expert. His vineyard had been home to several from the Civil War era. Until they disappeared a few weeks ago.

If there was anyone who could help me communicate with a ghost, it was probably him.

Trish took a bite of her pizza, stringy cheese stretching as she maneuvered the slice away from her mouth. She mumbled, "You like him, don't you? It couldn't hurt to talk to him."

"He's nice. But that doesn't mean he likes me. You remember what happened the last time."

"So, he got arrested." Trish shrugged. "That was your other boyfriend's fault."

I chuckled. "I just have the one quasi-boyfriend, thank you very much. I don't think Cyrus was interested in me that way. And you're right, it was their fault. Not mine. Do you think Cyrus is over it?"

"I think you should find out," Trish said. "He's lived for like, forever. If he holds onto grudges, they probably fit into one of two categories. Short, inconsequential things. Like this. Or centuries-long feuds—like with other beings who live forever."

"Good point," I conceded.

It was a good idea to at least talk with Cyrus, if only to cover my bases. Then again, he'd come here for help when his ghosts disappeared. So maybe he was as lost on the subject as we were.

I took a sip of wine. It tasted good. Earthy but light. I was never going to be a sommelier. Every time I heard someone rhapsodize about the hint of cherries or raspberries, or the notes of mushroom or whatever, I had no idea what they were talking about and I was thankful I didn't.

My mind was still on the girl and her book. "So, did I royally screw up today?"

"No, Constance." Trish shook her head. "This kind of thing happens. It's always awkward when they show up in the shop. I prefer phone calls. No, that's not true. I prefer when they get mailed in unannounced. Someone finds our address and ships a book here without my involvement."

"So, you've had something like this happen before?" I asked her.

"I think you mean have I lost a book before…"

"Sort of."

This bookstore wasn't Trish's livelihood. And that this particular book didn't necessarily matter to her as much as it did to me. But it would still be comforting to hear she'd made such a big mess of things, at least once. And maybe she could offer a solution—aside from waiting for the book to turn up online.

"I said it happens," Trish replied.

"And what do you do when it does?"

"I didn't say it ever happened to me."

I glowered at her.

"Okay. Okay." She put her hands up, defeated. "It happened to my mom a few times. And she took it personally. This shop was her life's work, you know. That's why I'm still here in Creel Creek. It's why I'm broke, living paycheck to paycheck. This shop means everything."

"I don't think your mom would care if you packed everything up. It's not like this is the best location." I inadvertently glanced at the vape shop at the end of the building.

"You're probably right," Trish agreed. "Anyway, what Mom did when something like this happened... she made a potion."

"Really?"

"They're not just for love," Trish said. "You can make a potion to put someone in any mood. You can make one to ease pain, to heal, to disappear. There's a potion for almost everything. But it's like this spell, we have to find it. It's not like there's one potion book to rule them all. And there's another problem..."

"We don't know where she lives."

"Oh, we can get that." Trish smiled. "Anyone who sets foot in here will have a trace on them for a while. Benefit of the wards I have on the shop."

"Then what's the problem?"

She played with the Triquetra pendant on her neck. "So, potions aren't really something you can sneak into someone's food or drink. Basically, if you mix a potion with something, it nullifies the effect."

"I've heard," I said.

"I never actually watched when Mom used them—only when she made them."

"So, you're saying we have to get some random person to drink a concoction without tricking her into it?"

"Oh, we can trick her into it. We just can't hide it in a margarita."

I thought about that. "Are you sure your mom tricked people into drinking the potion?"

"I mean, I'm not a hundred percent, but what else would she do?"

I had a different idea. My vast amount of Harry Potter knowledge was tugging at my brain, and it had been ages since I'd gone to a trivia night.

"She could have taken it," I said. "Your mom."

I explained that in *Harry Potter and the Half-Blood Prince*, when Harry needed to get a memory from Professor Slughorn, he took the Felix Felices potion. Liquid luck made almost anything he wanted happened for him. If there was a real potion like that, we could drink it. Or I could. And with luck, I could get the book.

"You know," Trish looked thoughtful, "that *does* make sense."

So that night, instead of searching for a spell to free Brad, we set out to find a potion to give us a little luck.

## 10

## IN WITCH I HAVE TEA WITH THE UNDEAD

So, how does one contact the god of the undead to have a chat about ghosts? I chose text messaging.

Cyrus agreed to have me over, at the vineyard the next day around tea time. I had to look up what time that was. Then I had to ask Trish for half of the afternoon off.

Not that I had anything to worry about there. Aside from our visitor with the book, it had been all quiet on the bookshop front for weeks.

We'd yet to find the perfect potion for luck, but we made a large dent in the potions section.

The next afternoon, I told Twinkie goodbye, flipped the store sign to CLOSED, and locked up. Then I pointed Crookshanks towards the other side of town, driving out to where just a month ago, we'd found Nell Baker's body in her cabin in the woods. Nell was another witch and even more an eccentric than Gran. She'd used her powers to lure evildoers to her cabin, then turned them into animals. That was a shocker. That day, we'd released several into the woods, including a possum that I'd briefly changed back into a man by accident.

I shuddered at the memory.

A few miles past that spot, the vineyard popped into view. Grapevines marched up the hill in rows up to the estate's house, all of it surrounded by secure fences. I punched the code Cyrus gave me into the gate, and it inched open. The driveway was long and circled a fountain. On my last visit, it had been empty. Today, clear water splashed from the tip into a clear pool.

The breeze sent mist spray in my direction, which felt refreshing in the heat of the day. In my head, I always thought August should be cooler than it is. But it's as much summer as July.

Cyrus met me at the door himself. He told me his usual butler, Lurque, had the day off. And just like my last visit, he led me to the dining room where a fine china tea service steamed, ready and waiting for us. There were several bottles of wine, unopened but available beside the plentiful assortment of scones and other pastries.

"Are you expecting someone else?" I asked.

"No. But my chef never does anything halfway. We're very much aligned in that way."

"I can see that."

For a casual meeting, Cyrus was dressed to the nines in slacks and a sports coat. His shoes were so polished I could see my reflection. His caramel skin glowed in the afternoon light streaming in the large windows. But his square chin and chiseled cheekbones were shadowed.

Cyrus had spent many years in Europe. In France, he'd learned wine. In England, he fell in love with a vampire. This vineyard was kind of a tribute to his many lives. Most of the decor had an Ancient Egyptian feel, gold and turquoise. Statues of all types were tucked away in every room. In the dining room, there was an oil painting the size of a Chevy, and if I had to guess the artist, the name that came to mind was Leonardo da Vinci or perhaps Raphael—someone from the Renaissance. To imagine, he'd lived through all of it, watching it all take place through his eternal lens as others grew old and died.

Cyrus had suffered several lifetimes worth of heartaches and pain. My problems were piddly compared to that.

"Do you have tea every day?"

"Most days," he said. "A habit from an earlier time. But it's usually not like this. You're aware I cannot truly digest food due to my circumstances."

I nodded. *Mummification.* I didn't know the exact specifics, and I'd never ask, though I pondered it often. Cyrus could sip tea. He could drink but not eat. I figured liquid could more easily slip through whatever was there.

He held his saucer with one hand and pinched the teacup with the other, not sticking his pinkie out. "Your text said you had some questions for me. I assume they aren't like last time. Not unless someone else has been murdered?"

"Uh, no. Nothing like that." I had trouble with the lie.

"Ah, but it is, isn't it?" He crossed his legs and gave me his undivided attention. "Who did I murder this time?"

"No one," I tried to play it off. "It's not like that."

"But someone *was* murdered. That much, I can tell just from your tone."

"My dad," I said. "We're trying to keep it as secret as possible."

"But how does one keep murder secret?"

"The police don't think it was murder," I told him. "Because he was murdered by magic."

"Well, magic isn't really my—"

"He showed up in my room as a ghost," I said so fast the

words were probably unintelligible. And yet, Cyrus managed.

"Ah. So, I'm the ghost expert now? You know, it wasn't too long ago I was in your shop looking up things on my own. Without any help from my local witches."

"I know." I sighed. "And I'm sorry about that. I really am. I was hoping that maybe you'd gotten somewhere. Maybe you've learned something that could help me."

"Help you do what exactly? Your father's a ghost. There's nothing you can do to change that. Be happy that you two can—"

"He's not a ghost anymore." I frowned.

Cyrus's face went flat. "Oh… I see. He crossed over. He moved on."

I nodded sadly.

"And you want to speak with him?"

"Just one more time," I said. "When I saw him that night, it was so rushed. And I was incoherent. I didn't have a shirt on. Don't ask. There are so many things I want to say."

"He knows them."

"There are so many questions I want to ask."

"I'm sure they can wait."

"How do you know that, Cyrus? You've never even crossed over. You don't know what it's like."

"That's where you're wrong, dear." Cyrus stood, took a peek out the window at the sun, still rather high above the mountains, and said, "Follow me. I'll explain."

Down the long corridor, every pair of doors opened to rooms equal in grandeur to the dining room. There was a formal living room, not a room with a TV, but something akin to what's found in the White House. A library with books shelved ten rows high with an attached ladder on a track called my name. At the end of the hallway, Cyrus opened the only single door.

I had an eerie feeling I knew where this went. The cellar, the place he kept his sarcophagus—where the podcasters had found him in mummy form.

I stopped abruptly, not wanting to move forward but I wasn't sure why.

"Nothing down there bites," he said. "I promise you."

I took a breath. "Right. It's not that."

"Do you trust me or not? If not, then come back another time. You can bring your friends. Bring Trish or Dave. Although I'm not actually sure which one I prefer."

"Right," I said again. "I trust you." I followed him down.

"I did die, you see," he said. "And I didn't stick around after my death. I wasn't a ghost. No, I had to be called back. I had to be found."

"Who found you?"

"Isis's familiar. A cat named Bastet. After Isis restored my body, he had to find me. Otherwise, the healing she'd done would've been for naught."

"I didn't think familiars could go to the afterlife."

"What if I told you that I'm the reason? The thing with rules is, you don't need them until you do."

"Oh." I didn't know what to say, so I found a question to ask him. "Did you want to come back?"

He stopped dead on the spiral staircase, turned around to look at me, and smiled. "That's a good question. The answer is no. Bastet had to come back three times with pleas from Isis before I agreed. And here I am centuries later, still not sure if I made the right choice."

"So, I guess you don't think I should try to talk to my dad..."

"That's not for me to decide," he said. "But I *am* telling you, the world will not end if it doesn't happen. Souls are meant to cross that plane. When they don't, that's when there's a problem."

The temperature had dropped as we made our way down, enough to make me shiver. A dehumidifier hummed somewhere. The wine cellar was a wine cellar, just how one might picture it. Stone walls, arched ceiling, reminiscent of a tunnel with barrels on one side and racks on the opposite.

What set this cellar apart from every other in the world was the enormous stone sarcophagus. Unmistakably Egyptian, carved with hieroglyphs on every side, the lid was completely covered in gold and painted to resemble Osiris.

"Did you ever find out what happened to the ghosts?" I'd meant to ask him much earlier.

Cyrus continued past his coffin without looking at it, but it was all I could see.

"I think that maybe I did," he said. "You know, legend calls me the god of the undead. But like many gods of the lowercase g variety, it's a title and nothing more. There's no weight behind it. I don't shepherd anyone to the afterlife, although sometimes I wish I did."

"Is this what you wanted to show me?" I touched the lid of the sarcophagus.

"Oh, no. Not that old thing. We had such a time getting it here, you know. It's traveled with me since my death. No, what I wanted to show you was this."

Cyrus went to the wine rack, found a bottle, and pulled it down like a lever. And like a lever, it clicked into place, releasing the wine rack to swing open like a door revealing a narrow threshold in the stone wall.

"Go ahead. Take a look inside."

"Do I—do I have to?" The last time I was at the vineyard, there was concern—mostly from Dave—that the invitation had been a trap. He'd suspected Cyrus of murdering the local vampire, Eric Caulfield. He was right to be suspicious, Cyrus had lied about who he really was. He and Mr. Caulfield had once shared a life together. Undead and undead. Undead and vampire.

"Just a peek," he said. "Remember, it was you who wanted to quote unquote pick my brain—which by the way is a weird saying, especially to someone who's had their brain pulled out through their nostrils. But never mind. Poke your brain in there and take a look."

"If I have to." I knew there wasn't a real threat. It was just my brain—inside my head and not out my nostrils—making something out of nothing. My witchy senses usually let me know if I'm in trouble. Lights would flicker on and off. My fingers burned. Nothing like that was happening. If Cyrus was going to lock me up in his cellar, my senses didn't have a clue.

I peered into the chamber. It looked much the same as the cellar but instead of wine, there were a few old cots. Not quite as ancient as the sarcophagus but old enough.

"I told you that the ghosts were from around the Civil War. However, I failed to tell you the whole story. They weren't soldiers. They were slaves. This house was part of the Underground Railroad.

"There was a skirmish—a small battle a few miles from here. And the Confederate soldiers took refuge here. All the while slaves slept under their noses.

"But that night, they were in for another surprise. Eric slaughtered the whole lot of them. He dragged their corpses to the battlefield. What he didn't know was one of the slaves had heard the noises. She'd snuck upstairs and seen everything."

"And she came back here?" I asked.

He nodded. "Her and a few others. They knew he wasn't a monster. They wanted to say thank you. The way things were—there was no guarantee they wouldn't be caught elsewhere and sent south. And as for why they all stayed, I think they wanted to be together. They'd been through the same things. They were separated from their families long before the war. While they were running, they became each other's family. And they stayed on even after death."

"But where are they now?" I asked.

"That's what I wanted to know. I thought maybe they'd just faded away like some ghosts do. But those are ghosts with no connections to the world. No, what I found out is much more interesting. Our ghosts? They made their own world."

"I don't understand."

"Do you know how the shadow realm works? Layer after layer after layer—almost like a multiverse but not. The multiverse is infinite versions of you splitting off and creating a new universe when you make different decisions —happening endlessly around every person who ever existed. The reality is, there's only one you, and she's standing right here.

"But the hereafter is a whole other beast. It splits from this world in infinite ways. Every person could have their own if they chose to. Most don't. They share worlds. But like a multiverse, those worlds change and split. Our ghosts figured out a way to create their own."

"How do you know this?"

"Because I have an inside source," he said. "Shortly after

our last little chat—after I was released from jail—another ghost appeared. I didn't believe it to be possible, but he found a way."

"Who?"

"Eric," Cyrus said, "you can come out now..."

## 11

## A NEW GHOST

From the patchwork of stone above us, the blurred legs and chest of a blue-tinted ghost descended into the cellar. He stopped beside Cyrus, hovering just off the floor.

"Hello, Constance," Mr. Caulfield said. "It's good to see you again."

I couldn't say the feeling was mutual. I'd only known Eric Caulfield a few weeks before his demise. And in those weeks, he hadn't treated me as I felt he should have. He was arrogant, chauvinistic, and overall, not a very pleasant person to be around. Add to that, I discovered his body. I was still recovering from that trauma.

Then what we'd discovered after did nothing to improve the overarching picture. I mean, he wasn't killing humans in the middle of the night or anything like that. He was operating an illegal blood bank and using the criminals Nell was keeping captive as the unwilling donors.

"Mr. Caulfield," I exclaimed. "You're back?"

"That's one way to think about it," he said snidely.

I didn't know any other way. If only he'd done it sooner.

He could've named his killer before all the crazy went down.

"It's a recent thing." When he was alive, I was always creeped out by how he seemed to know what I was thinking. It turns out he did. Now I wondered if a dead vampire could read thoughts like a live vampire—or whatever vampires are. (Dead undead?) One of their key abilities is to get into the heads of their victims. "And no, I'm not reading your thoughts right now. They're just written on your face."

*How could they not be?*

"How did you come back?" I asked. "And why?"

"I would think the why was evident." He glanced toward Cyrus.

Cyrus beamed. "Eric and I had a nice long chat when he came back. We really did love one another at one time. And we think we can again."

"As to the how," Mr. Caulfield continued, "well, it's not your concern. Let's just say reclaiming a soul, one removed for centuries, isn't for the weak of will. I managed."

"And he found the ghosts."

The nod blurred his ghostly face. "Strangely, I find the shadow realm easy to navigate. Once I got the hang of it."

"That's good." What else was there to say? Had Cyrus brought me here to see the hidden room or to meet Mr. Caulfield? Or both? I was so confused. Things had gotten off track.

I was no closer to talking to my dad.

"Well?" Mr. Caulfield asked, turning his ghostly head in my direction. "Are you going to ask me? Or are you going to let our past deter you?"

"What do you mean?"

"They were animals, Constance. I had to sustain myself somehow. Nell offered me a solution. You can't really be mad about that still."

*I'm not mad*, I thought. I wasn't anything. It wasn't the way I would've chosen to be a vampire. Then again, I didn't know the choices. Could one really be a "vegetarian" like the Cullens in *The Twilight Saga*? Could they live on pig's blood milkshakes like in *My Best Friend's a Vampire*?

The way he was talking, probably not.

"You're seriously not going to ask me, are you?"

"Ask you what?" I asked, frustrated.

"For my help," he said. "After all, I owe you one for catching my killer."

*Well, when you put it like that...*

I had no idea what kind of help he meant, but I'd take any.

"When the time comes," he said, "I can guide you to your father. However, I can't find him without you. But your souls are connected. With you there, it'd be easy."

So, once I was a ghost, he could help me.

*Thanks!*

I felt like rolling my eyes in Trish fashion.

Mr. Caulfield floated through a wall and out of sight. Even though I only worked with him a couple of weeks, I couldn't think of him as Eric.

Cyrus led back up the stairs. He insisted that I take wine with me—some for me, some for Trish, and some for Gran as well. He insisted. There was no politely declining them.

"And Constance," he said at the door, "you can pick my brain any time. But no prodding."

"Or yanking," I quipped.

"Oh, definitely not."

Curious and overstepping, I asked, "How does that work anyway? Did it get shoved back in?"

His smile was devilish. "You know, in all my years, no one has ever asked me that. No, it is not shoved back in. It's still in a jar—on loan to a prestigious museum at the moment. An enchantment links it to my body. It and *other* things."

"Gross." I smiled. "But also really cool."

"I think so too," he said. "And Constance, since you got to pry, I'm sure you will indulge me."

"Okay..."

"How are things with our local sheriff?"

"They're..." I struggled. "They're—"

"Slow." He nodded understandingly. "The man has a lot on his plate. A lot. If I were you, I wouldn't wait for him. If I were you, I'd go after what I wanted."

"Sage advice." I smiled, feeling as if maybe I'd found a friend, outside of Trish and Twinkie. "And thanks again for the wine."

I mulled over his words on the drive to Gran's and decided I couldn't wait any longer.

I called Dave.

"Constance, hey," he answered. "Is everything all right? There's not another magic trail to follow, is there?"

"Would you maybe want to go on a date?" I blurted the words. "And if so, are you free tomorrow night?"

Dave mumbled something incoherent on the other end.

"What was that?"

"I said I'm not free, not as of now. But I will be. I can be. What are we going to do?"

"I don't know," I said. "You pick."

As dates go, his picks were on the safe side. He mentioned dinner or a movie, which were about the only things Creel Creek had to offer, so I had to cut him some slack there. Besides, I'd put him on the spot. Honestly, I didn't care. I had a date with Dave Marsters, and that was plenty to be excited about.

## 12

## IN WITCH I GO ON A DATE

My hair had grown to the middle of my back. No matter how much care or product I used, it had gotten frizzy. The split ends had split ends. And no spell I tried had worked on it. I was in need of a haircut. I'd been in need for some time, but I kept putting it off. A stylist, a dentist, a doctor, and a good place to get a coffee or a donut—finding new places was the hidden cost that no one factors before they move.

The date with Dave forced me into action. I had to get a trim at the very least. Some color would be nice. But, my mostly-blonde hair hid the grays pretty well.

When I brought my up urgent need at the bookstore, Trish recommended her stylist. And though I wasn't a fan of her bangs or that strip of purple in her hair, my only other referral had come from an octogenarian. Gran's mop of white curls was another I wouldn't emulate.

But there were only three shops in town. The two I mentioned and one other. An unknown quantity.

That's why I ended up at a stylist that cut men's and

women's hair, with Trish holding my hand the whole way. Just not literally. We weren't *that* close.

She made our appointments, claiming that she, too, was in need of a touchup, pointing at the dark roots above her purple stripe.

Like Trish, the shop was edgy. The walls were painted black. Framed mirrors hung on the wall—they weren't built in, like I was used to seeing in salons. Upon entering, we were offered soda or beer from a cooler behind a chest-height counter.

"No, thank you though." I struggled with the idea of holding a beverage while getting my hair cut.

"She has a date tonight," Trish told the guy behind the counter.

"Ah, so you don't want to fill up," he said. "I get it. You know, I think I've got a bottle of wine back here. I wouldn't mind opening it."

I went to say no, but Trish shoved me aside with her hip before I got the chance. "That sounds awesome, Louis."

The name suited him. He had a handlebar mustache, curled with wax at the tips. He wore round glasses.

Trish shot me a maniacal look. "Don't give me any schtick about day drinking. It's been a long week. A long month. And it's not like it even matters to you," she alluded to my inability to get drunk.

"True," I replied. "But I didn't sign up to be designated driver either." Trish's yellow bug was a stick shift—something I hadn't driven in well over twenty years. I'd never owned one, but Doug, one of my boyfriends from undergrad, had insisted I learn on his truck. Both the relationship and his driving lessons ended badly.

Louis found some red cups and divvied the wine up between us and a few of the stylists—or barbers. *Whatever.*

As we waited for ours to finish their appointments, Trish chatted with Louis.

It wasn't only the salon's décor; every stylist gave the same vibe. They had tattoos and piercings. Some had gauges in their ears. Mine had a lip ring. Her name was Ruth. Tattoos were scattered across her pale arms, and she had a large dreamcatcher on her thigh. Her hair was a normal shade of brown, highlighted with lighter shades and some blonde. Today, she had it French braided into two pigtails. She was young and cute, wearing cut-off shorts with some cheek showing. Some was more than enough in my mind—that was a style I'd never dream about trying, but Ruth pulled it off. I wondered why Trish hadn't chosen her for herself.

Trish's stylist was a guy with a shaved head. And on that head, he had an old-school tiger tattoo, like something a sailor might get. He had more, from his neck down to sleeves—tattoo sleeves, not shirt sleeves. His knuckles advised, *Hold Fast*. His beard could have been tucked into his pants. In a town like Creel Creek, this guy screamed warlock. But I wasn't going to say that to his beardy face.

The only warlock I'd ever met lived up to the reputation Trish told me about. A bad one. Anyway, I doubted if Trish would trust a barber that dabbled in the magical arts. But then again, he did have a pentacle tattooed on his shoulder.

"So, whatcha thinkin?" Ruth asked. She feathered out my hair before combing it, checking both of our reflections in the mirror. It felt strange to see myself again, even though it had only been a week since Gran took our mirrors down.

I shrugged. "Like this but shorter, I guess."

"That I can do. Maybe two inches?" Ruth showed me her guess-timate of two inches with her thumb and pointer finger. It looked okay to me. "And how about color? When

Trish booked you, she said she didn't know, so we reserved you the whole time slot."

"Oh, I'm sure she knew what my answer would be."

Ruth suppressed a smile and nodded toward the wine in my hand. "Maybe she thought liquid courage would say something different."

*If only*, I thought. There'd been a few times over the past couple of months that I'd wished alcohol could give me anything—including courage.

"Not today," I said.

"Come on! Live a little," Trish called. A strip of aluminum foil was already twisted around her usual purple streak.

"I think pink would look really good," Ruth offered.

My stomach got that queasy feeling, as if I was about to make some life-altering decision—like adding a strip of pink to my hair was some permanent change I could never come back from. Almost like getting a tattoo. Except totally not. Even so, those butterflies made the decision for me.

"Not today," I said again.

A few hours later, with my hair two inches shorter and straightened, I waited by the door to get picked up like it was prom night. In place of a gown, I wore a simple dress and some heels I brought out of retirement. I could never truly get the hang of them, but usually after a few steps I was able to achieve some grace.

Dave pulled up into the driveway. He'd traded the police SUV for his white minivan. Which, oddly enough, was a lot like my junior prom, when Terrance King borrowed his mom's Dodge Caravan with the wood paneling.

Dave had on a navy checked, long-sleeved button-down shirt, dark wash jeans, and leather shoes. I was still getting used to him without the mustache—his thin lips and slightly long nose. Of course, almost all of his face was covered in shadow, it being after five o'clock.

"Don't look in the back." He opened the door for me.

"Why not?"

"Because I didn't have the time to clean it. And even if I did, they don't make a vacuum that'll pick every single Cheerio from that floor."

Despite his warning—or perhaps because of it—I hazarded a look. It wasn't nearly as bad as he thought. The girls had restricted their messes to food, more or less. Only a few forgotten toys were tucked beside Kacie's car seat. Elsie had a booster, a tad cleaner. Allie, his oldest, either took the front or claimed the farthest back seat as her own.

We chatted about nothing on the drive from Gran's to Orange Blossom's, one of the few restaurants in town. It was the only chain, sporting locations across Virginia. The other restaurants in town were mom and pop establishments, all dating back at least twenty years or more. I hadn't had a chance to try all of them, but the ones I had were better than Orange Blossom's.

Here I was, already being critical. Not a good sign. Why was I questioning Dave's choice? Maybe he liked the variety on the menu—or he thought I would. Plus, they had a liquor license. Not that it mattered much to me.

*Sigh.*

A chipper hostess led us to a table in the far corner of the restaurant, well away from most others. The low lighting surprised me. Even the hokey chain restaurant radio could hardly be heard. "Did you have to pay extra for this spot?" I asked him.

"I slipped her an Abraham Lincoln when you weren't looking." He winked. "I know you're probably used to a lot fancier than what we have to offer here."

"Maybe."

"From what I've seen on the Food Network, all the restaurants out in California have Michelin stars. Here in Creel Creek, we're just lucky it doesn't serve Michelin tires."

"Good one." I smiled. "I'm guessing that's not your first dad joke. But honestly, I've eaten at some really good food trucks too."

"You know, I have too. The taco truck that parks out by the hospital is pretty dang good. Have you ever had it?"

I shook my head. Being from Southern California, I didn't think testing the local Mexican cuisine would be fair to anyone. Mostly myself.

"Well, next time you're in the area, you should. They have this ten-dollar combo—it comes with a Coke and everything."

"Well, if it comes with a Coke, I guess I have to, huh." I smiled.

We continued like that, then both of us ordered burgers. It seemed like the safest bet. I'd ordered a steak on my last visit, and speaking of Michelin, Dave wasn't wrong.

I got a margarita to wash the burger down. After the wine at the barbershop, I felt like something sour and sweet and totally different. Even without the temporary alcohol immunity, I would've had trouble getting a buzz. The amount of mixer involved was criminal, although Dave decided not to press charges.

"I know I'm terrible at this," he said after a while. I was feeling just as self-conscious. Dating is always hard. It's one of the few things in life that time and practice make you worse at, not better.

"You're not—"

"I want you to know that I know I'm terrible," he continued. "But I plan on getting better."

"And how do you plan to do that?" I ribbed, trying to sound flirty, not judgmental.

"You know, that's probably where this whole thing breaks down. I do not have a plan."

"Things were easier twenty years ago, huh?"

"You got that right." He sighed. "You know, there were still payphones around the last time I had a first date. Not many. But still. Payphones."

I knew Dave's wife had died of cancer a couple of years ago.

He studied the table, picking at his napkin. "I mean one time I went for coffee with a friend of a friend. I didn't actually know it was a setup—cause I'd been refusing those on principle."

"What happened?"

"Once I figured out what was going on, I paid for our coffee and faked getting a call from dispatch."

I feigned surprise. "Dave Marsters! I didn't peg you for that type. Now, I'm going to wonder every time you go to the bathroom."

"The same goes for you." He grinned. "What about you? Have you dated? If I remember correctly, you're not actually divorced…"

He was right. My divorce from Mark was still a couple of months away from being finalized. I could tell that didn't sit right with him, deep down. But Dave brushed it off quickly.

"Before Mark," I said, "all I did was date."

"Aside from your *other* marriage, right?"

I gaped. "Gran told you about that?"

"Trish. Something about a weekend in Vegas."

"We didn't sign the paperwork. It was just some Elvis impersonator thing. And please, can we not talk about it?"

"Sorry. I didn't mean to—"

"No," I said. "I brought it up. It's okay. And you're doing fine by the way."

He wasn't.

"As I was saying—" I took a sip of my sour mix. "—before Mark I dated a lot. Never anything too serious. And after Mark, I came here. This is officially my second date. Both have been with you."

"I'm honored." He brightened. "Have things changed much since you and Mark got together? I don't know how long you were…"

"Married? Not long. Only three years. But I never used any apps or websites or anything like that. So, I guess things are kinda the same."

"The whole game changed on me," Dave said. "In my day, I had to make time for long phone calls—which I don't even think this generation even does anymore. Seriously, I remember having to block Imogene out so she couldn't get the phone before my call. Sisters!" He rolled his eyes.

"I always wanted one."

"Yeah, well they're okay most of the time."

"What were your dates like?" I asked.

"I know it'll be hard to believe, but Creel Creek used to have things worth checking out. Main Street was nice. There was goofy golf with batting cages and a go-cart track. It closed down and became the Creel Creek Credit Union. They paved right over it all."

"Sad," I said.

"Yeah. I'd go on three, maybe four dates in a week. And sometimes, if I played my cards right, there was a sleepover in there too. I mean, I do still have sleepovers, but they've kinda lost their luster." He grimaced. "Three girls and me in a king-size bed. It happens more than you'd probably think."

"Sounds cozy," I offered with a laugh.

"Oh, it *is* that. I get this tiny sliver at the edge. Kacie ends up in the middle, all sprawled out. Her sisters don't seem to mind though."

"Do you braid hair?"

"Oh, I'm terrible. No amount of YouTube videos can teach me. I lose track so easily."

I smiled. "It sounds like every slumber party I've ever been to."

"Well, we should do it sometime." He straightened, then blushed, realizing his mistake. "I mean with the girls—like camping or something. I didn't mean—"

"It's okay," I said. "I know what you mean. And I'd be okay with the alternative too."

Those words just slipped from my mouth. And once they were gone, they were out there.

He blushed an even deeper shade of red. "Yeah, uh, that sounds good. That sounds great." He was at a loss. I grabbed his hand before it could touch his beer and wrapped my fingers around his thumb, squeezing him reassuringly. He didn't chance moving it again, not even when we ordered a slice of cheesecake and he had to slice forkfuls with his non-dominant left hand.

The night ended in Gran's driveway. Dave turned the headlights off. We kissed, not thinking about time and not rushing anything.

## 13

## IN WITCH I'M HEXED

The next morning, I had coffee with Gran while Stevie lapped milk out of a bowl. His throaty hisses filled the room as he tried and failed to warn the other two cats away—the *real* cats.

We laughed.

"I hate drinking after them," he boomed. "If you only knew where those tongues have been."

He was all talk. I'd caught him snuggling up with them enough times to know that he cared for Purdy and Tabatha. Purdy was white with large black spots on her back and freckles on her legs like a Dalmatian. Hence the name. If I were to compare Tabatha with a dog, the only breed that would come to mind would be mutt. Her coat was shades of black that turned to gray, shades of brown that muted to orange, the long hair shaggier than the carpets in a 70s porno. All of the carpets.

Stevie sprang onto the kitchen table where Gran let him have some coffee from her cup.

"Now it's *your* tongue with the questionable past."

"If you want to know about tongues, you should talk to

Constance," Stevie said. "I think I saw her using hers last night."

I choked.

Gran eyed me. "Yes, how was your date?"

I never knew what to say in situations like this. When I was in high school, my mother wasn't there to talk to about dating. I had no one to commiserate with when they went badly or to gush to when everything was perfect.

Dad refused to believe I went on dates. In his mind, his daughter was on her way to being a nun. She went out with friends—to movies, to dinner, to park at that isolated construction site on the other side of our subdivision. Maybe he didn't know about the last one.

"It was just a date." I shrugged. I had to tell myself that too. Just one date. Better than our first but still awkward. Dave and I were from two different worlds. Two different people. And we were two different types of paranormal—not that it mattered.

Dave had already settled down. He had kids. I'd just settled... for Mark—a liar and a cheater and an all-around terrible person, someone nowhere near the bar of what a husband should be.

Inside, I knew that Dave had hurdled that bar already. *But is he the right guy for me?* There was only one way to find out, and that might require more terrible meals at Orange Blossoms.

"Just a date, huh." Gran harrumphed.

"She doesn't like to kiss and tell," Stevie offered.

"So, there was kissing?" Gran asked.

Stevie nodded his cat head. "With tongue."

"There was a kiss," I said. "And gross. Why were you watching? Don't you have better things to do? Isn't there a certain job you're supposed to be doing with your spare time?"

"No. My spare time is mine to do with as I please. I do your and your grandmother's bidding when I'm on the clock, as they say."

"On the clock?" I scoffed. "What—do y'all have a union now?"

Stevie tilted his head to the left and gazed at me through yellow eyes. "You realize I'm doing you a favor, right? Several, in fact."

"I'm sorry," I said earnestly. "It was a joke. I'm still allowed a few of those, aren't I? I'm just not a fan of either of you prying into my love life."

I did feel bad. He was right. He was doing something, only I couldn't keep tabs on him. I was starting to feel overloaded. It felt like I wasn't doing enough to solve my dad's murder or bring Brad back. There were too many things to keep track of. To many familiars. And now a ghost. It felt like managing a software product—a job I wasn't keen to go back to.

"I never pry, dear," Gran lied. If anything, that was all she did aside from watching television. Speaking of, it was almost time for the *The Price Is Right* and my shift at the bookstore.

I showered and dressed and put on a dab of makeup, but like the night before, I had no mirror. So, when I got into Crookshanks, I twisted the rearview around to peer at my reflection. Only, something was off. My eyes were red, not the blue eyes I was used to. It looked almost like I'd put smoky eyeshadow on the bags under my eyes. And my crow's feet were jagged lines cut into skin.

When I looked again, it was me—the one I was used to seeing. *A trick of the mind?* My witch inclinations often did things like this—changing my perspective, on people, the environment, and even myself.

Ten years before, it would've been this reflection that would've caused me to pause. The lines on my cheeks, the sag under my chin. At least my makeup looked okay.

It was a short drive to Bewitched Books, most of which was highway. And even though it neared ten o'clock, Crookshanks was the only car on the road.

The sun was above the trees on the east side of the road. The layer of morning fog that usually stretched across town was already baked away by the heat.

The air conditioner struggled to do more than blow hot air in my face. The car was old. I'd gotten it in grad school—a gift from Dad. Through everything I'd been through these past several years, Crookshanks was the constant.

We were about a mile away from the *Welcome to Creel Creek* sign when I lost the feeling in my hands and feet. They didn't go numb. There was just nothing. I could still see them—see that they were working, but I couldn't feel them. I tried to will my head to turn, but it wouldn't move.

Then I leaned right and looked into the rearview mirror again. Only, I didn't force that movement. It wasn't me moving my body.

The reflection. I could see the other face staring back at me. It was the same sinister me from before. And she winked.

The engine revved—Crookshank's protest against the foot on the accelerator. My foot but not my actions. The speed crept higher and higher, peaking at eighty-eight miles per hour.

*Am I going back in time?*

She looked in the mirror again, sinister me. I wanted to shout. I wanted to scream. She didn't let me. She put a finger

—my finger—to her lips and shook her head. "Nah, ah ah," my own voice said.

She tore our eyes away from our reflection, making me look at what she did next.

I no choice but to watch.

My hands jerked the wheel. First left. We swerved. Then hard to the right. The wheels lost traction. And maybe it would have been okay had we not touched the grass. Suddenly, the car was airborne. At that moment, I could feel again. Feel my hands and my feet and everywhere else.

I could also feel that sinking in my stomach as if I were on a roller coaster. And I wish that was the last thing I'd felt. The car rolled once, twice, three times, coming to a stop upside down at the edge of a ditch. The car was crushed around me. The airbag had popped me in the face like Muhammad Ali. And something sharp found my calf. And while I was thankful to be strapped in and not flying out the windshield, my seat belt had squeezed the air out of me.

I only had a second or two to think about what just happened but I really didn't care to. For me, it was over. In that moment, I knew I was going to see my dad again. And I was happy.

Less so when Dave's voice woke me up, in a hospital bed with every single part of me aching. I've never been through childbirth, but I had to imagine that this was what it felt like. Except this pain wasn't localized—it went from the top of my head to my toes.

## 14

## UNBINDING

"Do you remember what happened?" Dave put his hand over mine and squeezed gently.

Only yesterday, we'd done that on a date. Today, he was in uniform, all brown and khaki, his hat in hand. His short dark hair had been flattened by the cap except for a cowlick.

He wore a grim expression on his handsome face as he looked me over. His eyes went up and down my body—but not in a good way.

He let go of my hand far too soon, then started twisting his hat anxiously.

My right eye decided to stay closed. My calf throbbed.

Dave tried to smile. It wasn't especially reassuring. "Constance, do you know where you are? Why you're here?"

"I had a car wreck." It sounded more like a guess than I meant it to.

He nodded. "Your Gran and Trish are out in the waiting room. They're worried sick—we all were."

"Sorry," I said, as if it were my fault.

"The doctor says you're going to be fine," Dave said.

"You're just a little banged up. Okay, more than a little. Cuts, bruises, and you've got a few cracked ribs. So, try not to breathe too deeply."

"Is that it?" I tested my lungs. It wasn't my best idea ever.

"What? You want there to be more?" He shook his head and his smile was real this time. "I'm just wondering what kind of animal you saved by swerving off the road like that."

"It wasn't an animal," I said.

Dave stepped back and checked the hall, probably for the doctor. I took a moment to get my bearings.

The room was small, just big enough for a bed and a couple of those uncomfortable chairs. The whiteboard below the TV listed the names of my doctor and two nurses.

"If I'm fine, then what's all this?" I raised my arm about half an inch. It was all I could manage with the blood pressure cuff, the IV line, and the doodad on my finger checking my pulse.

"It's standard operating procedure," Dave said. "If you're comfortable in this place, you're either visiting or you're dead. Which, honestly, might well have happened. You were lucky we got you out in time—you have Willow to thank for that."

*Willow's psychic abilities to the rescue again.*

"When we found your car," Dave was saying, "the sight of it… I… Well, I thought the worst. Then seeing you… Constance, I don't think you want to look in a mirror right away."

His words triggered my memory. "I need to see Gran and Trish."

"There'll be plenty of time for that when—"

"Now!"

"Okay." He stopped twisting the ball cap and put his

hands up in surrender. "Now it is. But you need to take it easy. All right?"

"Says the guy who went back to work a week after getting shot."

"That guy has special healing abilities," Dave said. "Last I checked, you don't."

"Actually," I said, "Trish and I found a potion for that just the other night."

"I don't suppose y'all made any?"

*Busted.*

I went to shake my head but pain shot through my back from the base of my skull. And I realized that funny feeling around my neck was a brace. No moving allowed.

"Yeah, I wouldn't try that if I were you," Dave said. "I'll be right back with the whole Scooby gang."

After they got to my room and everyone stopped fussing, I explained what happened in the car—the face I'd seen in the rearview mirror, my body being controlled, and what I remembered of the accident.

"You must've been hexed," Trish said.

"Maybe. Maybe not." Gran kept looking me up and down like Dave had. "Possession and hexes often look the same."

"You think she was possessed?" Dave asked.

"Don't rush me. I'm mulling it over."

"I guess it *could* be possession," Trish conceded. "But I don't know much about demons. Do you?"

Gran pursed her lips. "I've never called one up myself," she said. "I've known a few witches who have—Hilda and your mother included. They almost always regret it."

Dave arched an eyebrow. "Wait... you actually call demons up? Like from hell?"

"Not *the* hell," Gran denied. "That place is outside our

purview. These demons live in the shadow realm. Unlike other spirits, they're locked there."

"Until someone," Trish added, "usually a witch, unlocks the door by summoning them to Earth."

"To do what?" Dave asked.

"Mischief of one sort or another," Gran replied. "Demons usually specialize. There's a range. Some might trip you on the sidewalk. Others will give you nightmares. And a few will eat you whole."

"And everything in between," Trish added.

"Great," Dave lamented. "So, some demon is on the loose and has picked Constance as its target."

"Demons rarely get loose," Gran said. "Even on Earth, they're usually bound in circles—held by magic to do a witch's bidding. If it was a possession—and I'm not convinced it was—then there's still a solid chance that someone is behind it."

Gran peered down at me through her bifocals. Then she inched closer and closer to the bed until finally she reached out to touch me. I flinched in anticipation of pain that never manifested—at least no more than I already had.

I wondered what she was doing—or more specifically, what she was touching.

Gran gently lifted a lock of my hair, inspecting the ends as she twisted the strands between her thumb and forefinger. "When was this cut?"

"Yesterday," I said. "Wait, you didn't notice?"

Gran dropped the hair and stepped back. "I said you looked good for your date."

"Right. New hair. Some makeup. A dress. High heels. I thought you noticed."

"I saw the whole picture, not the fine details."

"I just want to say," Dave put up a hand, "that I noticed.

It looks great."

"Sure you did." Gran frowned. "Did you go to my shop like I told you to?"

I remembered this time not to move my head. "No."

"She went to mine," Trish's voice sounded meek. She hunched up, ready for the smackdown.

And she got it.

Her eyes narrowed, Gran snapped, "Does this shop of yours know how to properly dispose of hair?"

"It's a regular shop. I think they sweep it up and throw it away."

"You mean everyone there is *normal*?" Gran asked her. I couldn't help but picture how not quite normal they were.

Trish said, "Normal in the mortal sense of the word. Yes."

"And they just sweep it up in a dustpan? Drop it in a can?" Gran folded her arms.

"It's actually this cool vacuum thing—"

"Trish Lester! I know your momma raised you better." Gran waggled her gnarled finger. Only, for a witch like Gran, this was like pointing a gun. "We can't go disposing of our hair where anyone digging through a bin can find it."

"What does this have to do with my hair?" I finally asked.

Dave added, "I was wondering the same thing."

Trish and Gran wore identical horrified faces.

Then Trish sighed. "It's one way to get yourself hexed. If you have someone's hair, their nails—or especially their blood—you can bind it with a doll or even with yourself, which might've been done to Constance. Anyone who has them can control you. I'm sorry. I wasn't thinking."

"You can say that again!" Gran looked like she expected Trish to say it again.

"Constance, I'm really, really sorry." Trish hung her head. "This is my fault. Listen. I'll brew that healing potion tonight and bring it here first thing tomorrow."

"A one and done healing potion?" Gran asked.

"We found it the other night. It should be sufficient for her injuries."

"I really don't need a potion," I chimed in. "I'll be out of here in no time."

They looked at me, all three of them.

"What?"

"You haven't seen the doctor yet, have you?" Trish asked.

Dave shook his head.

"You haven't seen a mirror either," Gran added.

"Constance, it's pretty bad," Dave said gently. "The, uh, the air bag did a number on that lovely face."

I knew my head was throbbing, and my eyes hurt. I'd kept the one shut for most of our conversation. When I tried to open it, my nose was more visible than normal. These were things I was willing to look past—literally—while we figured out what had happened to me in the car.

"It can't be that bad, can it?" My heart raced.

"Should I get her a mirror?" Trish searched the room.

Gran shook her head firmly. "There'll be no more mirrors."

So, I didn't see what my face actually looked like. But at a guess, I had a broken nose and probably two black eyes. The left side of my mouth was swollen. It buzzed with that numb feeling you get from a shot of Novocain, which it turned out I had. Because I was missing a tooth—my left incisor. At least I wouldn't be mistaken for a vampire.

On the whole, I'd been lucky. It was just like those silly Subaru commercials. Crookshanks was totaled. And someone could look up and say, "She lived."

In fact, once I took the potion Trish made for me, I walked away almost unscathed. Aside from the tooth, which I had to visit the dentist about. Another new friend.

But that was after I took the potion. Nothing could've prepared me for how a potion goes down. It's not like drinking foul-tasting water. Not like drinking sour milk. And not even like downing a glass of cod liver oil—though that comparison is more apt.

The potion had the look of greenish-brown slime. Thinner than sludge but thicker than oil. Trish told me to put the glass to my mouth, not to think about it, and allow the contents to find their way to my stomach.

Only, the potion didn't take the straightforward path that gravity offered. It acted as if my esophagus was a maze. At first, I couldn't breathe. Not even through my nose. Then I tasted it. The texture of an earthworm mixed with the taste of raw mushroom. Then there was fire. Burning my insides to the outside. From my lungs to my skin. Finally, cool water filled my stomach like I'd opened my mouth and drunk from the bottom of a waterfall. Then it was over.

I never wanted to take another potion. Or at least, that's what I told myself. But after a few minutes, the memory faded and I began to sense the healing effects.

It really was like having a baby—or so I've heard.

The doctor discharged me the next day—after my "miraculous" recovery. His words.

And that night, Trish came over to Gran's house for dinner. We had a lot to discuss. I hadn't told either Trish or Gran about the new ghost in town, Mr. Caulfield. Then there was the circle of witches coming up that weekend, in conjunction with the crescent moon—where we'd originally hoped to out the culprit.

Things were more complicated now. Whoever killed my

dad also had to be behind my hex. Which meant they also had to know that they'd gotten to me. And seeing me alive might be a surprise. Or even worse, they might try to finish the job.

We listed our suspects, each as unlikely as the next. Our witch neighbor Agatha. The graveyard was in her backyard too. Hilda Jeffries lived across town. And there were two more witches closer to my age—Lauren Whittaker from Charlottesville, and Kalene Moone whom Gran didn't care for much.

Of that group, we knew the least about Lauren. But Gran's suspicions of Kalene trumped everything.

"If there's a turncoat in our midst, then I'm sure it's her."

"But why?" I asked.

"Well, I guess it boils down to her mother," Gran said. "She never liked me much. I don't know why."

"Mmm... okay." Trish arched an eyebrow.

"What? I never did anything to her. I never sent a curse her way. Or a *hex*," Gran emphasized. "But I know I rub people the wrong way sometimes."

"Yeah, just *sometimes*." I smirked.

Trish and I exchanged knowing looks.

"I was going to say it might've had something to do with *your* mother," Gran said. "Rainbow—that's Kalene's mom—she visited here not long after your mother took that job with the Faction. It was just before she disappeared—or before I knew she disappeared."

"What'd she want?"

"I don't remember," Gran mumbled. "And after that, she wouldn't have anything to do with me—or us. She hardly ever attended a circle after that."

"Why?"

"Like I said, I don't know." Gran turned nasty. "But I do

know that Kalene hung on her mother's every word. And when her mother died, she changed. She wasn't the same girl I'd known for those forty years."

"She died before Kalene became a witch?" I asked.

Gran nodded.

Trish and I both turned solemn. Neither of our moms got to see our fortieth birthdays either.

"How?"

"She was in the courthouse the night of the fire."

"Wait." I frowned. My Creel Creek knowledge was limited. But I passed by that courthouse every day and thought I knew the history. "I heard that fire was sixty years ago."

Gran shook her head. Trish too.

"That was the first fire," Trish said. "They moved the courthouse, but they kept a few offices in there. Rainbow worked there for quite a while."

"What'd she do?"

"Bookkeeper," Gran said. "Just *not* like you two."

"What was she like?" Trish asked. "Was she like Kalene?"

"In what way?"

"You know," Trish shrugged, "in *all* of the ways."

Gran considered the question. "No, not like Kalene at all. She was a mighty powerful witch. Mighty powerful."

"But if she was a powerful witch, how did she—"

"We all die, Constance. That is the one certainty in our lives—they come to an end."

"Okay," Trish said, not wanting to stay on *that* subject long. "You say Kalene's inept. Would the Faction really recruit someone like that?"

"Did I say inept?" Gran asked. "I meant dimwitted."

"Is there a difference?"

"Well, the first would mean she's incompetent, which

she isn't. She knows things—things about magic and how it works, even if her skills are lacking. The latter means that she's a little dense in the ways of the world. There's a word for it in school."

"Book smart?" I asked.

"That's it!" Gran patted her knee. "She probably didn't know any better. She got mixed up with the Faction and she—"

"And she got in over her head," I finished.

"There's a slight chance she didn't even know what she was doing with that spell," Trish offered. "Or who she was killing."

"That's true." Gran nodded. "It could've been one of those initiation type things. Do this to get in our order." Gran said sarcastically.

Trish frowned. "She *has* always wanted to join a coven..."

"This was the next best thing," I said.

"Perhaps even better in her dimwitted mind. See!" Gran pointed at Trish. "I say dimwitted, not the other."

"I'm pretty sure you've said both."

"Anyway"—Gran scowled at Trish—"we won't know anything until Saturday night, which leads to our next dilemma."

"Which is?"

"The hex," Gran said. "We have to break it before you get killed—or worse."

I didn't want to think about what she meant by worse.

"I thought about that too," Trish said. "Will a spell break the binding? I don't know of any. But I did think of one solution." She winced. "I don't think Constance will like it."

"Not a spell," Gran answered. "The fastest way to unbind this hex will be to break the circle that's woven with the hair. We need to cut it." Gran jerked her head toward me. "Then the connection's with a pile of mess on the floor and not to you."

"We should probably burn the hair too," Trish added. "Just in case."

"Agreed." Gran made a decisive nod as if the matter was settled.

My vision tunneled. "You two are scaring me. What does that even mean?"

"She means we're going to have to shave your head. Like with a razor." Trish watched me with interest, waiting for my reaction. She smiled wickedly when the realization dawned on my face. "You're going full G. I. Jane."

While I was partial to Ellen Ripley in *Alien 3*, I much preferred keeping the hair on my head—all of it. I covered the top of my head in a futile effort to protect the blonde locks from such a fate. "You're kidding, right? Y'all are joking with me? There's gotta be a spell."

"I wish we were," Trish said. But neither she nor Gran were very convincing. There was an eager gleam in their eyes. They thought this was kind of funny. And it probably would've been, had it not been my hair.

Gran was already rummaging in the junk drawer for a pair of scissors. But before she found them, Trish pulled something from her purse.

Clippers.

"I told you," she said. "I'd already thought of something."

She flicked them on, and they hummed the iconic hum heard in barbershops around the globe.

My stomach dropped to the floor.

## 15

## IN WITCH I WEAR A WIG

"How long does it have to stay like this?" I traced my finger over my scalp. The bare skin was cool to the touch and more textured than I could've ever imagined. "Am I allowed to let it grow back?"

"You can start growing it out now, if you like," Gran said. "Losing your connection with it is what mattered most. The goings on in your follicles is of little importance."

"That's right," Trish agreed. "That hair is no longer a part of you." She pointed to the piles on the floor. "So, it won't identify with you. It's just hair now—with no power over you."

"So, it *is* like G. I. Jane," I said. "This was about empowerment. And I took my power back."

"No. *We* took it back," Trish said.

I couldn't stop touching my head. "I think the other witches are going to suspect something when they see me this weekend."

"Good point," Trish agreed. "We need to get you a wig."

"I've got several in the closet upstairs," Gran offered.

And if I wanted to look like Dolly Parton in the Eighties, I would've taken her up on that. Trish and I found something decent online—one that looked more like my normal hair and rush ordered it.

And it's what I wore that Friday before the crescent moon, my first day back to work since the accident. It was oddly comfortable, kind of like wearing a beanie.

But while I had a temporary replacement in the hair department, there was no replacing Crookshanks. I had to borrow Gran's Buick until the insurance money got squared away. And I'd yet to hear anything about Dad's insurance or a sale pending on his house.

Gran had spelled the mirrors away, making it harder to drive that boat of a car than it already was. Side mirrors were probably required by law. Luckily, I knew someone in law enforcement who promised not to pull me over.

I hadn't told Dave about my hair. He'd tried to visit me at Gran's, but I'd thwarted him, telling him I wasn't feeling well.

The potion had done its job and then some. I felt ready for a marathon. My body coursed with newfound energy. And I had a new appreciation for potion making. I'd spent those days at home with books, looking for a luck potion.

Even with a potion there was no guarantee that Mr. Caulfield's help would mean speaking to my father again. If he was merely a go-between, that wouldn't fulfill my need. I wanted to speak to my dad again, no matter what it cost.

The familiars continued their search for Brad, which felt more and more like a lost cause.

Familiars are much more than protection from the shadow realm. For instance, Trish and Twinkie had a whole system for tracking the books that had passed through

Bewitched Books over the years. This system relied on Twinkie's encyclopedic knowledge of every witch that had ever set foot in the shop and what tome she left with.

I wasn't there more than ten minutes before Twinkie left for the shadow realm. And I wasn't there ten minutes more before Dave came for a visit. I couldn't turn him away from an open store. Furthermore, he was likely to be the only customer that week, but by the looks of him, not a paying one.

"You know," he said, perusing the mystery shelves, "except for that *one* time, I've never been in here."

The time he was referring to he'd been in his wolf form—and not on purpose. I shuddered. That was a side of him I could never get used to.

It wasn't as if he could control it. I'd read so many books when I was younger that played it like witches and vampires and werewolves were different species. Like if I married a werewolf, I was doing some sort of crossbreeding. The truth is, we're all just humans at the core.

"So, uh, you don't read?" Maybe we *were* different species.

"I read—we read. The girls love books. There're several shops in Charlottesville. I just never think about this place when it comes to books. I guess it's because I know what it *really* is."

"It's more than that," I countered. "It's still a used bookstore. We have a lot to offer."

Sure, Bewitched Books was mostly stocked with paranormal reading—books on the occult, about ghosts, and pagan rituals. But the other half of the store was like any other used bookshop. Yellowed mass market paperbacks got dusty on the shelves. A few times a month, our regular local customers traded their lot for another batch. They didn't actually patronize the store as much they rented a few books a month.

"Well, now that you're working here, I have more incentive to stop by," he said. "But if I'm honest with you, I listen to a lot of audio in the police car. Don't tell my bosses, all right?" He mumbled the last few words.

"Who are your bosses?"

"I'm looking at one of 'em. The taxpayers are who I report to—technically, at least. But if I could, I have a question for you." Dave scratched the stubble on his chin and studied my face. "I can't figure it out. I know there's something different about your hair. But for the life of me... Did you get *another* haircut?"

I sighed. I knew this would come up eventually, but I wasn't about to take off the wig and show him. I told him everything though.

He smiled. "I'm sure it looks fine. You have one of those faces."

I arched an eyebrow.

"You know. Just one of those faces. One that looks good no matter how you wear your hair. Like... like Demi Moore."

"Please, don't make that comparison again."

"Why?"

"Because I'm not a Hollywood actress. Growing up in Southern California, I got a little jaded by that crowd. It weirds me out when women look better at fifty than they do at twenty-five."

"Eat right. Exercise."

"Get a load of Botox," I finished.

"Okay." He blinked. "I won't compare you again. Just know that I think you're gorgeous. And I've been thinking a lot about that conversation the other night. Like a lot. I was out of line. I never meant to suggest—"

"A sleepover?" I smiled but quickly hid it. There was still the missing tooth to contend with next week. Demi Moore never had one of those.

"Yeah, a sleepover."

"I knew what you meant. And I really do love your girls. If they want to do something like that, just have a girl's night, I'd be game."

"You would? You're serious?"

I nodded and smiled without showing my teeth. "We could lock you in your room and watch a movie or something. We can braid hair. Well, not mine."

He chuckled. "I think they'd like that. It's been too long, ya know. Imogene does her best, but her boys take up most of her free time. Are you free this weekend?"

"Not this weekend." I shook my head, glad it didn't hurt like the last time we'd talked.

"You got better plans?"

"Not better. A pagan ritual in a graveyard. Probably not something they'd be interested in."

"Well, you never know. I mean, the things Allie gets into these days"

"You're a good dad," I told him.

"I try."

"So, I guess you aren't worried at all?" He began scanning the mystery shelf again.

"What's there to be worried about? Besides a witch trying to kill me. Obviously, I'm worried about that."

"I am too," he said. "Constance, if we find out who did this to you, they're going to pay a hefty price."

"Dave. You don't have to—"

"You were hexed. Almost killed. Where I'm sitting, that's attempted murder."

"I get it," I said. "But don't be so chivalrous. I can stand up for myself."

"I know you can. Let's talk about the fact that Jade and Summer could be staking the place out after seeing us there. I wonder if they have it bugged or something."

"You're the sheriff," I said. "Can't you search for bugs?"

"Oh, so *now* you want my help? Not with murderers, with podcasters." He sighed. "Their podcast is mostly harmless anyway."

"Mostly," I agreed. "But you're right. I think being cautious is smart. I'm sure there's a spell I can cast to make sure they aren't around."

"Good. You should do that." It looked like he might go but then he found a book. Agatha Christie. "Here's an old friend," he said.

I told him to take it.

He struggled a moment before saying, "What about next weekend? For the sleepover, I mean. We'll have some time before the full moon, so nothing to worry about there."

"How does that actually work by the way?" I asked him.

"Shifting into wolf form? I thought you saw that."

"No." I shook my head. "With the girls. Who keeps them?"

"They stay with a sitter, Mrs. Mitchell. Another shifter—not of the werewolf variety. The moon doesn't normally affect her. And she can shift at will. One of those types. The boys—Imogene's boys, that is—they stay with her too when the need arises. When Jared can't manage. He's a—"

"Let me guess. Another shifter?"

Dave nodded. "Yeah. We aren't sure what the boys are

yet. Part werewolf and part coyote. The next few years should be interesting at their house."

"Okay. Well, if you ever need someone else, I'm available."

"Thank you." He smiled. "Really, Constance. Thank you. I think this is gonna be great."

## 16

## CRESCENTS, CIRCLES, AND CONSPIRACIES

On a cloudless night, the crescent moon high and bright in the midnight sky, seven witches entered a graveyard and climbed a hill. Or more accurately, we trudged up a hill, allowing the slowest among us to lead the way.

And that wasn't Gran.

It was our neighbor Agatha, who was in her mid-to-late seventies. Agatha had long gray hair that she kept in a bun. She wore a pair of glasses on a chain around her neck, though I'd never seen her use them. Maybe they were for reading.

And next to her was Hilda Jeffries. An African American woman somewhere between my age and Gran's, she was the tallest after me. On my birthday—when I'd come into my powers—she was the one who'd gifted me immunity to poisons, having built her own immunity to them over several years building her tolerance by ingesting poison. This was somewhat similar to the way Westley in *The Princess Bride* built his tolerance to iocane powder.

Trish and I helped Gran, who managed things like stairs

well, but the long grass on the hill was slick with dew. The two younger witches, Lauren and Kalene, trailed behind us. Lauren was a cute forty. She was one of those girls who looked she never aged a day, at least not since she was fifteen. Her dark hair was cut to chin-length, and her bright blue eyes were round, taking in everything and everyone, usually with a smile.

Kalene, on the other hand, looked her age. Fifty. She was short and on the dumpy side. She huffed and puffed more than anyone when we stopped at an elderly oak on the top of the hill.

As trees go, this one was climbable. Its branches reached out in all directions, even down the slope of the hill. There was a spot—one branch—I could hop on and climb up. And like a kid, every time we were here, I fought the urge to try.

From the top of the hill, the clearing gave way to the forest beyond it, becoming a shadowy sea of leaves. I stood there a moment, staring. There was something—something I'd forgotten or forgotten to do. I struggled, trying to focus on what that was.

"You okay?" Trish asked.

"Not really. I forgot something."

"You leave your broom double-parked?"

"If only." I wished we were allowed to use brooms; it would've made the trip here at lot easier. And I'd gladly use it instead of Gran's Buick—which I complained about to Trish every chance I got.

Still, I couldn't shake the feeling I'd forgotten something. Something important.

"I'm sure it's nothing." Trish shrugged it off.

"It's been a while," Lauren appeared between us. "I hope everyone's doing okay. I heard about that wizard who, uh, tried to take your powers." Lauren made a face in my direction, her bright eyes asking me to elaborate.

Commuting from Charlottesville meant she wasn't privy to the local gossip.

I thought I probably should add her to a group text or something. Kalene and Hilda too. As it was, the older generation could get behind. Gran and Agatha were hopeless.

"He was a warlock," Trish replied.

Gran harrumphed. "And he wouldn't've tried to do it had *she* not been nosing around in that vampire business."

"I wasn't nosing."

"Yeah," Trish agreed. "She wasn't nosing. We were doing our part to help local law enforcement."

"Well, I know why *she* does it." Gran indicated me. "Why do you?"

"Boredom." Trish sighed. "And he was my boss."

"Well, if I were you two," Hilda Jeffries interjected, "I'd stop putting my warts where they don't belong."

"Warts?" Kalene asked.

"You know, like warts on a nose," Hilda said. "It was a witch joke."

"A bad one," Gran said. "And what do you know about these two putting their warts where they don't belong?"

"Nothing much." Hilda pursed her lips thoughtfully. "I just heard they were at Nell Baker's place when her body was found. You know it's bad luck to find a dead witch."

"Fenny snakes," Gran spat. "It's bad luck to find anybody dead—whether it be a witch or a vampire or just a plain old human."

"Is that why we're here tonight?" Lauren asked. "Because someone else died?"

Lauren was an observant one. Maybe too observant.

"Something like that," Gran nodded. "Now, most of you

know I'd never accuse any of you here of doing anything like murder."

"There's a but coming," Agatha interrupted.

"There always is with one as large as yours." Gran scowled at our elderly neighbor—who did have a rather large behind. "If you're gonna keep interrupting me, we're gonna be here all night. And by the look of you lot, you could all use some beauty sleep."

"Sorry, Jez," Agatha told Gran. "I won't interrupt you again."

Gran frowned and picked up where she left off. "You know that I've seen a lot of things in my day. A lot of magic. But I'll be the first to tell you that I don't know everything about it. And I've been guilty—as I'm sure you all are—of performing a spell without knowing its true power."

"Who got killed?" Kalene, who'd just caught up to the conversation, asked.

"I'm getting to it," Gran huffed. She turned to me expectantly.

"My father," I said. "He was murdered by a killing curse." We'd decided to just come out with it given the other circumstances—my being hexed.

"Like in the movies?" Lauren asked. "Like Harry Potter?"

"Not exactly. But I traced the spell to this spot. Right here by the tree."

Several of the witches instinctively stepped back and scoured the area around the tree like the magic or its facilitator were still here. And maybe they were.

"We're not saying anyone here did it," Gran lied.

"But aren't you?" Hilda snapped. "Honestly, Jez. Why would we come here to the circle if we did it? You think we're *that* dumb?"

"Yeah," Kalene agreed. "That makes no sense."

I tried to calm them down. "Gran thinks that maybe whoever killed him didn't know that's what they were doing. It's just a spell. Maybe they didn't know…"

"If that's the case, what did they *think* they were doing?" Hilda put a hand on her hip. It was a good question. One I didn't have an answer to.

Trish played with the pendant on her necklace. "It's possible they were told to do the spell by the Faction."

At that name, everyone went quiet.

"Like *the* Faction?" Agatha was the first to speak.

"The one and only." Gran nodded.

"I haven't heard that name in years," Hilda said.

"What's the Faction?" Lauren asked.

Kalene was quiet. She shrugged in Lauren's direction.

"If you don't know then your presence in this conversation is moot," Gran said.

"Well, thanks for the invite. It's been real," Lauren huffed. She turned to go.

"She did drive all the way out here," I said.

"I'm a part of this coven too," Kalene spoke up. "I think you owe us a better explanation."

"It's not a coven," Gran said firmly, then she called to Lauren. "Fine. Fine. Come on back."

Exasperated, Gran explained what we knew about the Faction. The little we knew. Hilda and Agatha chimed in from time to time, nodding along until we got to the parts about my mom and me asking around about her.

"So, you think they're trying to cover something up?" Hilda asked when I was done.

"Maybe."

Kalene shook her head. "Why go through the trouble, though? Couldn't they just kill *you* and be done with it? No offense."

I took some offense; they *had* tried to kill me. I was about to say as much when Gran shot daggers in my direction.

"This organization"—it was Agatha who spoke—"they don't like spilling witch blood. Not unless they have to. But I still don't see how this has anything to do with us."

"Someone used this graveyard to perform the spell," Gran said. "Who but one of our own would do such a thing? Why not use their own sacred ground?"

"To make a point—just like you said," Hilda replied. "You know it wasn't one of us. And we could've had this conversation anywhere. And not during the witching hour."

"Well, you're here now," Gran said darkly. "Constance is going to cast a spell on the tree. It will allow her to see the color of your magic. One at a time, place your hand on the trunk."

*A spell.* That was it. I was supposed to have done a spell. I was supposed to have checked the woods for Jade and Summer. I'd forgotten.

I peered out at the inky horizon. It was already too late now. If they were there, they were there.

"And if we don't want to put our hand on the tree?" Agatha asked.

Gran did nothing to conceal her displeasure. "Then we'll have to assume you're guilty... of something."

"I was just asking, Jez. I'll put my hand on the tree."

"I will too," Lauren added. She turned to Kalene, who shrugged.

"Sure. Whatever."

"Do your worst." Hilda was the first to put her palm on the trunk. "My opinion is that this is a waste of time. But I've been wrong before."

I recited the spell Gran taught me, then I stretched out and touched the oak with the tip of my index finger.

Instantly, Hilda's hand began to glow with orange light. She pulled it away, and where her hand had been glowed for almost a minute before fading into the trunk, the tree absorbing the magic.

"What color did you see?" Trish asked.

"Orange," I said. "The rest of you can't see it?"

They shook their heads.

"Okay. I'll go." Just as she'd told me when we searched the original trace, Trish's handprint glowed a vivid green like her eyes.

Agatha's trace was ruby red.

Kalene was next. Oddly, I could barely see her magic. A faint glittery blue color flickered and was gone, almost like her magic was fading.

I didn't have much time to reflect on it.

"Well?" she asked.

"It wasn't you," I said.

Gran took a turn. She pressed the bark and yellow sparks flew, leaving a golden outline on the tree.

"I guess it's my turn," Lauren said hesitantly. It's always hard to go first or last.

At this point, I was confident of what I'd see. Nothing. Hilda was right. This had been a waste of everyone's time.

Lauren closed her eyes and reached out.

Then a twig snapped below us.

"Crap! That was me," someone hissed loud enough for us to hear.

We looked down the hill at two shadows running through the gate and into the edge of the woods.

"Who the heck is that?" Agatha asked.

"Podcasters," Trish grumbled.

"That's not good," Hilda said. "Not good at all."

I nodded my agreement.

"What'd I miss?" Lauren opened her eyes, which had been closed during the brief commotion.

"Nothing mu—" I'd turned in Lauren's direction just in time to see purple magic—the exact same color as the trace—shimmer and fade into the tree.

## 17
# CREEL CREEK AFTER DARK EPISODE 54

It's getting late.
Very late.
*The creeping dread of tomorrow haunts your dreams.*
*It's dark out. Are you afraid?*
*Welcome to Creel Creek After Dark.*

**Athena:** I'm your host, Athena Hunter.

**Ivana:** And I'm Ivana Steak. We're back for another special episode.

**Athena:** All of our episodes are special, Ivana.

**Ivana:** While that's true, they aren't usually recorded live on location—if you know what I mean.

**Athena:** I think I do. There was only that one, a couple of months back. So, you're right. Tonight's episode is special. It was recorded mere hours ago as the two of us encountered a group of what we believe to be witches. And what were they doing? They were gathering at midnight in a freaking graveyard!

**Ivana:** Tonight's episode is brought to you by the fine

folks at Treebeard's Trail Cameras. Hidden in synthetic moss, give your tree a beard that's *also* a camera.

**Athena:** Their motion sensing technology can send notifications straight to your phone. Anytime there's activity, you'll know—which is how we caught on to this gathering tonight.

**Ivana:** Treebeard's Trail Cameras. Find them locally at Wicked Hunting Supply.

**Athena:** Without further ado, let's get to the show.

*Microphone crackling.*

**Ivana:** This is Ivana Steak. And we're whispering again. You know what that means.

**Athena:** It means we're tracking something down. But *not* Bigfoot.

**Ivana:** Sasquatch.

**Athena:** Whatever. It's not the big guy. It's actually several smaller citizens of the local community. We caught them on our trail camera moving toward the graveyard on the outskirts of town. This is the same graveyard we mentioned in episode thirteen about the mine explosion. Ivana, this could be where your ghost hangs out at night.

**Ivana:** No. He hangs out at Creel Creek Mountain Lodge.

**Athena:** Oh, right. Well, anyway—we're following the trail of these women who came out here just before midnight tonight.

**Ivana:** Kind of an odd time to have a picnic, don't you think?

**Athena:** Yeah, and I don't think this is a Junior League meeting either.

**Ivana:** What do you think they're up to, Athena?

**Athena:** Well, the last time we were up this way, we'd heard mention of the word magic—no matter what the

Hound says. So, I believe these women are what we might call witches. Now, let's go get a better look.

**Ivana:** Okay. We're about to reach the clearing and try to get a better look at what they're up to. We'll be out in the open for a bit.

**Athena:** Why didn't we put the camera on that tree?

**Ivana:** The one in the graveyard?

**Athena:** Obviously.

**Ivana:** Well… I guess because we didn't think of it?

**Athena:** Curse our past selves.

**Ivana:** Don't talk about curses. You never know what these witches are capable of if they spot us…

**Athena:** I'm afraid if we talk too much, they'll hear us.

**Ivana:** Me too. But we made it to the gate of the graveyard. So far, I don't see any hint of magic.

**Athena:** But what I do see is odd. They're taking turns putting one hand on the oak tree.

**Ivana:** Maybe it's an initiation ceremony?

**Athena:** It's definitely some sort of ritual. Come on, let's get a closer look. We can duck behind those gravestones.

**Ivana:** I am not ducking behind a gravestone. Summ— Athena, wait!

*Crack!*

**Athena:** Crap! That was me.

**Ivana:** Run!

**Athena:** Sorry, folks. I stepped on a stupid stick. Right when it was getting good.

**Ivana:** What'd you see up there?

**Athena:** Their faces.

**Ivana:** And we're back from the recording. Now Athena is going to tell us what or who she saw.

**Athena:** Our suspicions are confirmed, Ivana. The

Bookish Witch is *definitely* a witch. And surprise, surprise, so is The New Girl.

**Ivana:** Should we change her name to The New Witch?

**Athena:** I'm not sure—because there was a face in there I didn't know. And a few others I did.

**Ivana:** Who?

**Athena:** Well, I've thought of names for all of them. Together, it's like: The Head Witch, The Ancient One, The Harpy—

**Ivana:** Wait... The Harpy?

**Athena:** You know. She sings with that blues band on Friday nights down at Earl's Bistro.

**Ivana:** Oh, right. And the others?

**Athena:** They were The Bookish Witch, The New Girl, The Mystery Witch, and The Hag.

**Ivana:** Clever. But what does it mean?

**Athena:** It means, Ivana, that everything we've ever thought about Creel Creek is true. All that's left is to prove it.

## 18

## IN WITCH WE REFLECT

I was rooted to the spot, just like the tree beside me. Dumbfounded, I questioned if I'd really seen what I thought I'd seen. Or had my mind played some trick?

*Can more than one witch have the same color magic?* Surely, they could. This had to be a coincidence. It just had to be.

I couldn't speak. I couldn't say a single word to Lauren after seeing the purple outline of her hand on the tree.

I took a deep breath and stumbled a few feet down the hill when my legs crumpled beneath me.

"Is everything okay, Constance?" Lauren asked, apparently oblivious, without an ounce of malice or suspicion in her bright blue eyes.

"It's fine," I answered. "I'm fine."

Everything was not fine.

The other witches started down the hill. I tried to follow but I didn't have the energy, not until Trish pulled me away by my wrist.

"Let's get out of here," she said, "before the Wonder Twins come back."

At the clearing, we split into different directions. Agatha

toward her house, Hilda, Kalene, and Lauren toward the cemetery where they'd parked their cars as usual.

Trish went with me and Gran. We met Twinkie and Stevie, who'd been waiting outside the graveyard gates. As usual during the witching, their shadows flickered between their familiar body and other, more sinister shapes.

The woods were quiet aside from the hoot of an owl. Since moving to Creel Creek, I'd been followed by an owl. It went everywhere with me, even during the day. I'd seen it swoop across the sky behind my car. I was sure the same owl had scooped a bat with its talons in the graveyard on midsummer night. Of course, that bat wasn't really a bat. It had been a human man, a warlock, before I transfigured him.

Quietly, we made it into Gran's backyard.

"Constance," Trish said, breaking the silence, "you want to tell us what that was all about?"

"We tried to prevent them," Twinkie interjected, her deep familiar's voice a shroud enveloping the air. "I ran over their feet a few times. They didn't even notice."

"And they tried to pet me. 'Here puss, puss.'" Stevie raced through the cat door, perturbed. As I'd learned when the grocery store was robbed, familiars are for warning and protecting witches from the evil elements in the shadow realm. They're pretty useless when it comes to other mortals.

Trish scooped Twinkie into her hands, and we followed the cat inside.

"So, these were those women from that radio show you talk about?" Gran asked us.

"Podcast," I corrected.

"I thought you said they weren't anything to worry about."

"They aren't really," Trish said. "I know they aren't. We just have to be better. We should put up wards so they can't see into the graveyard."

"Trish Lester!" Gran said. "That's one of the best ideas I've heard. How come I didn't think of it?"

"I don't know. Why didn't you?"

Gran pursed her lips and shrugged.

"Okay, that's settled," Trish said. "But it wasn't what I was asking Constance about." She leaned against the counter in the kitchen.

"Then what were you asking about?" Gran put the kettle on.

"I was asking Constance what—what she saw up there."

In the walk from the graveyard, I'd done my best to push my thoughts aside. They came rushing back. unsteadily, I took a seat, suddenly shaking. My arms and my legs went numb.

"I saw Lauren's magic," I said.

"And?"

"And it was the same color as the trace."

"You're sure?" Gran asked.

Trish pushed off from the counter and rushed to my side, offering an arm around my shoulder. "Why didn't you say anything? We could've done something."

"I don't know. It all happened so fast. I just couldn't."

"You're sure it was the *exact* same color." Gran was still hung up on the details. "It wasn't another shade of purple?"

"What are the odds of them being the same?" Trish asked Gran.

"I'm a witch, not a statistician. I know magic. If the color was one decimal different, just slightly off, Constance's witch inclinations would tell her so. If she thinks they're the same, then they are."

"You don't really think it was Lauren, do you?"

The question was for either of us. Me or Gran. I decided to answer. "That's the thing... I don't. More witch inclination. That's why I couldn't tell her. Between that and Jade and Summer, it wasn't the right time."

"Maybe she was used," Gran offered. "Maybe she was hexed just like you were. But instead of wrecking a car, she uttered a spell."

"That has to be it." Trish nodded her agreement.

"But wouldn't she remember it?" I asked.

Trish shook her head. "Probably not. I mean, we wiped all those people's memories at the Midsummer Festival. This witch could've used the same spell. Then Lauren's none the wiser."

"And a murderer," Gran said.

"Do you think we should tell her?"

"Definitely." Trish squeezed my shoulder. "I'd want to know."

But Gran scowled. "Or you could have your friend Dave talk to her. He's used to that kind of thing."

I sighed. "None of this is even in his jurisdiction. And he doesn't know much about magic."

"And you do?" Gran took the kettle off as it began to whistle.

"Trish does. You could come along too..."

"Oh, no. I'll let you be the true detectives." Gran shook her head. "I hate to third wheel when there's perfectly good TV to watch at home."

"I can't tell if she's joking," Trish said.

"She's not."

Gran smiled thinly. "I am what I am. And I'm not one to meddle."

"Now, that's a lie," Stevie piped up.

Trish smiled at me. "And I thought you got your daily allotment of sarcasm from me."

She put Twinkie on the table. Gran dunked bags of chamomile in the mugs before doling them out. I squeezed a healthy dose of honey into my tea and sipped until my hands stopped shaking and I'd regained some composure.

Trish allowed Twinkie to help herself from her steaming mug. Stevie leapt onto the table where Gran let him to do the same. Stevie and Twinkie got along fine as familiars. It was only when his feline nature took over that we had to be careful. As a general rule, he wasn't fond of rodents—neither were the two real cats, but they hid when company was over.

"She's not overt with her meddling like you two," Stevie continued. "Jez is more a spy at heart."

"I came of age during the Cold War. But not the one you're thinking of," Gran added.

"I don't think it's a grand idea." Twinkie sat on her hind legs and joined the conversation. "Confronting another witch without any proof."

"The magic is the proof," Trish argued.

"It's still one witch's word against another's. What else do you have?"

"Nothing." I sighed.

"And where will this confrontation take place?" Twinkie asked.

"I know where she works." Trish said. "Yeah, we should definitely go there."

"On her home turf?" Gran shook her head. "Her rules. What could possibly go wrong?"

"We're just going to talk to her," I said. "Unless..."

"Unless she's the real killer," Twinkie said. "You never

know. Maybe tonight was a ploy to lure you in. A small one, I know—but it seems to me it's working."

"Speaking of," Trish said, "don't the two of you have some other work to do?"

"Right. We do."

Stevie left and the mouse skittered down the leg of the table, then across the floor. She climbed through the cat door with some effort.

"Well, I'm not going to say another word," Gran said.

We stared at her. Usually when someone says something like that, it's followed with a "but."

Gran just took a sip of tea and shrugged.

"That's it? Really?"

She nodded yes. She looked tired—tired as anyone who'd stayed up six hours past their usual bedtime.

"If you're not going to say another word," Trish said, "then I guess it's time I go." She stood and put a reassuring hand on my shoulder. "Listen. I know tonight didn't go well. I don't think it fractured our circle, but I could tell it put a bad taste in a few mouths. Twinkie's right, we can't go around accusing other witches of things."

"Isn't that exactly what y'all plan to do next?" Gran asked.

"I thought you were done talking."

Gran scowled, and Trish relented. "That's what I was going to say. We can't make this seem like an accusation. I want Constance to come up with another explanation. Anything else. I'll pick you up first thing Monday morning."

Even though it was late—even though I was tired and in desperate need of sleep—I spent the night awake with my thoughts. I was cursed. I was hexed. And I was over it.

## 19

## IN WITCH WE GO FOR A DRIVE

Trish pulled into Gran's driveway around the time I'd normally head to work—except Bewitched Books was closed on Sundays and Mondays. Not that we had to worry about customers anyway.

She'd taken the day off—which was probably for the best. I couldn't imagine how awkward Jade and Trish's next meeting would be.

In their work capacities, they were manager and assistant manager of the grocery store. Outside it was this strange contest. And now Jade knew what we did late at night. Whether she really thought we were witches, or we were just playacting in the woods, was up for debate.

It was Summer—Athena on the show, who believed. She was also in it for the wrong reasons—she hoped to leverage the show's popularity to become rich and famous. *Good luck!* I could only think of a handful of podcasts that ever made it to mainstream culture. Even then the hosts were unknowns.

Still, every listener of *Creel Creek After Dark* was a threat to our paranormal community. And we couldn't be so heedless again. We'd have to ward the graveyard—and be careful using magic.

The yellow bug sputtered black smoke as we blasted off up the highway toward Charlottesville. We passed farmland and crossed through mountains. The view outside the window was serene and picturesque. Trish and I chatted again about the crazy events of Saturday night, listened to the latest episode of the podcast—of which we were the stars—and drank copious amounts of coffee we'd picked up for the road.

"So, where does Lauren work?" I asked. The signs for the city and the University of Virginia had just popped into view.

"Oh, you'll see." Trish eyes darted over, checking my reaction.

"I don't get it. Is it a joke?"

"It's an inside joke. And right now, I'm the only one on the inside—and I'm savoring it. You brought your driver's license, right?"

"I did."

"And your insurance card?"

"It's on my phone," I said, flustered.

"And I brought your last pay stubs. So, I think we're set."

I was beginning to get an idea of where Lauren might work. And I was right. Trish swung the car into the first car lot in sight, which just so happened to be a Subaru and Volkswagen dealership.

"You're kidding me."

"What? Witches gotta eat. What'd you expect?"

I shrugged. "I don't know. It's a college town. I thought maybe she owned a shop like you. Maybe she sold incense or tarot decks or something."

"Don't get me wrong," Trish said, "I like a good tarot

deck. But no cards are going to tell you the future. No crystal balls either."

"I get it. And no Magic 8-Ball."

"Oh, those were real. Now, concentrate and ask again."

"Is that *another* joke?"

"Signs point to yes." She yanked the parking brake up and shut off the engine. "Seriously, I think this is a win-win. We get some information and you take a look at new cars. This is where I bought this gal." Trish patted the dash.

"Was this before or after she joined the circle?"

"After," Trish said. "I think Hilda invited her originally. She met her doing new car shopping."

"Has she always lived here?"

Trish shrugged. "I guess we'll have to ask her."

We walked through the sea of new cars. "All of these have mirrors," I observed.

*Captain Obvious—that's me.*

"Good thing your gran isn't the only one who knows magic. Come on, the first bottle of water is on me."

Inside, the dealership wasn't really buzzing. There was a couple seated at an open table in talks with a man in a polo shirt and khakis. "This isn't the price we agreed to last night," the husband said.

"Sure it is," the salesman argued. "It's just we didn't account for your trade. See. Right here, we knocked two thousand off."

"I'm talking about the sticker price," the man said, raising his voice. "It's five hundred dollars higher!"

"Can I help you?" A receptionist at a circular desk in the center of the sales floor waved us over.

"Lauren Whittaker told us to come by," Trish replied.

"I'll tell her you're here."

A few minutes later, Lauren peered through an office

window with a dubious expression. She took a sip of soda from her desk, then she rushed out to greet us. "Constance? Trish? To what do I owe the pleasure? Wait... are you here to buy a car?"

"No," I tried to say.

"Maybe." Trish's voice overruled mine.

"Really?" Lauren looked skeptical. "You're sure this isn't about last night?"

"What do you mean?" Trish asked her.

*She must know*, I thought. But if she did, why hadn't she said anything then?

"Not here," Lauren whispered. "Let's go look for a car. Take a test drive, and we can talk in private."

She took my license and made a copy, then steered us in the direction of a new Subaru Outback.

*Poor Crookshanks*, I thought. It wasn't like the car caused the accident. And these newer models didn't even look like wagons anymore.

"You said you'd like a Subaru, right?" Lauren asked.

"No, I said I owned one."

"Oh, well, what happened to it? They hold their value really well. If you wanted to trade it in."

We'd skirted those details at the gathering in the graveyard. And now, in the light of day, I felt self-conscious about the wig. It had to be easier to tell in the daylight.

"She had a wreck," Trish stopped Lauren. "A bad one. This would be a replacement."

"Oh." Lauren nodded. "Right. Right. I'm sorry to hear that."

She gave me the keys. I looked at Trish. "Are you sure I should drive?"

"Everyone is wary about getting back on the road that first time," Lauren said.

I shook my head. "I can't do this. We might as well tell her the whole story."

"Only after *she* spills what *she* knows." Trish glared at Lauren.

"Okay." Lauren put her hands up, defeated. "Let's just get in the car. I can pretend I'm showing you the features."

"Oh, you're gonna do that too," Trish said.

We got in the car. I turned it on. Already, I could tell the A/C worked a thousand times better than the A/C in Crookshanks.

"What did you mean about last night?" I asked her.

"This is about me and Kalene, right? And Hilda."

Trish was taken aback but recovered quickly. "That's right. It's about you three."

"It's Kalene's idea, really. The whole coven thing, ya know. She's been on it for ages. But after last night... I'll be honest. That was weird. We were upset. Ya know—because you basically accused us of murder."

"I'm sorry," I said, not feeling sorry.

Trish rolled her eyes. "So, she wants y'all to join a coven? That's it?"

"Right." Lauren nodded. "I don't even know what that really means. My mom was never a member of a coven. I like the circle—when we're doing fun stuff like on your birthday. I had this idea, to do potion nights. I was telling Kalene about it a few weeks ago. I'm really into potions right now. She even loaned me a few books. In fact, she kind of gave me an idea—I'm thinking about starting a business."

"But what about last night?" I asked.

She sighed. "If you guys don't want me to join—or if you want to join us—I'm happy either way. I'll talk to Kalene for you. I'm sure with an apology, she'll understand."

"Lauren," I said, "we're not here about any of that."

"You're not?"

"No. I was hexed. That's how I lost control of my car." I took off my wig, revealing a very bald, very white scalp. "We think they used my hair to do it."

She gasped. "Do you think it's the same person who killed your dad?"

I nodded. "I think so. Yeah."

"If only you knew who performed that spell," she said.

She was as clueless as Cher Horowitz. A tear streaked out of my eye and down my cheek.

"The thing is," I said. "I do."

## 20

## DOUBLE DOUBLE TOIL AND TROUBLE

"That's—that's impossible."

"Why is it impossible?" Trish asked her.

"It just is." Lauren leaned back against the headrest. "Remind me again the day—I mean, the night—your dad *actually* died. What was the date?"

I reminded her.

"I wasn't even here. Not in Virginia, technically."

"Where were you?"

"In D.C." Lauren turned to face us. "That's why I remember the date so clearly—because I wasn't anywhere near here. I was in our nation's capital."

"Doing what?" Trish asked her.

"I was at my mother's funeral."

"Oh... wow. I'm sorry."

"Yeah. So I remember everything about that weekend. I think I'd know if my memory was wiped."

"You wouldn't." Trish rolled her eyes. "That's kinda the point."

"But would I *still* have memories of everything? My dad's poem reading. My brother's hot tears against my cheek. I can even tell you the food we ate that night. Then you're saying I somehow made my way back to the graveyard to cast a spell? That's a three-hour drive. And I woke up in my old bed the next day. So, how do you account for that?"

"I don't know." Trish groaned. "I'm losing steam here, Constance. Do you have any ideas?"

I shook my head. "Lauren, we're not saying you're a cold-blooded killer. But if you have ties to the Faction, you need to tell us."

"I never even heard about them until Saturday night," she said. "And can we at least go for a test drive? My boss in there is watching us. It doesn't take this long to run through the features."

"You still haven't done that by the way," Trish said.

"Just drive." Lauren exhaled sharply.

"You're sure this is safe?" I asked Trish, not chancing a look in the rearview. "It's still got mirrors."

"That's not how it would work anyway," Lauren huffed. "You can't just look in every mirror. Whoever's hexing you has to know where to look. Which I doubt would be in a random Outback at a car dealership in a town you don't even live in. Just saying."

"That's a good point," Trish agreed.

"Unless we were followed," I said.

"We weren't. There were no cars behind us for like half that drive."

That might've been true about cars, but my friend the owl swooped past when we stopped for coffee. But I knew in my gut its presence was a welcome one. It meant me no harm.

"So, let's blow the popsicle stand." We were barely out of the parking lot when she threw up her hands and said, "I can't fathom any of this. You actually think *I* killed your dad."

"We don't *think* that," I told her. "We *know* your magic did. I know."

Not knowing where else to go, I headed for town. Charlottesville was charming. It had a quaint downtown mall about as different from Creel Creek as it could be.

Lauren beat the dash. "That's it. My magic."

"What about it?"

"Someone—or something—must've stolen it."

"That's possible," Trish said.

"It is! With a demon," Lauren continued. "I was making a potion last week and it said for more potency, I could call a demon. I'd have it use its finger to stir—which is kind of gross from the get-go. But there was a warning. It said to be careful because some demons have the power to steal a witch's magic."

"Are you telling us you summoned a demon and *it* stole your magic?"

"No. I'm not *that* dumb. I'd never call one. If you make a mistake with your circle, you're done for. Some demons can take you to the shadow realm and hold onto your spirit forever."

"They can?"

She checked the side mirror. "Make this turn here."

Trish poked her head between the center console. "Okay. So, it could've been a demon. Or, maybe, someone else. Who all was at your mother's funeral?"

"My family," she said.

"Right. But are they like us? Any other witches? A vampire? Anything?"

"Just muggles. I don't have any aunts. The witching line

ran through my mother... and me, I guess." She trailed off, staring out the window.

I smiled at the Harry Potter reference. I believed her. I believed she wasn't there that night—that there had to be an explanation for her magic being in that trace. Anything besides her being a cold-blooded killer working for the Faction. My witchy instincts were telling me both—that it was her magic, and that I could trust her.

Which sounds confusing, but it wasn't. Not to me.

"You're sure, you can't think of anyone?" Trish asked.

"Of course."

"We're asking because Washington D.C. is supposed to be the stronghold of the Faction," I said.

"Then you'd think I'd know about it. I only lived there half my life."

"You did?"

She nodded.

"Why'd you leave?"

She sighed. "It's complicated. It involves a guy and bad decision-making. And the fallout. I'd rather not get into it."

"We're already into it," I said.

She sighed again. "Listen. My mother wasn't the nicest lady. She was a good witch, but not a good mother. We had an argument. And honestly, her funeral was the first time I'd been home in probably twenty-three years."

"And what was this argument about?" Trish asked.

"It's deeply personal," Lauren said. "Nothing to do with a demon or a Faction or whatever."

"Okay." I nodded. Again, I was beginning to trust her.

Lauren dug in her purse and slipped on a pair of sunglasses. "Kalene left these in my office when she gave me the book. Possession is nine-tenths of the law, right? Take this turn. This is where we show people the all-wheel drive capabilities."

I pulled into what amounted to an abandoned lot. A crumbled building where an old factory had been partially leveled. Its foundation and about two quarters of graffitied wall sat toward the back edge of the property. It reminded me of the outer shell of the courthouse in Creel Creek.

Grass was encroaching on the concrete but was sparse in the rest of the lot, which was made up mostly of dirt. Across from the building, there were a few small sandy hills in what looked much like a dune buggy track.

"What is this place?" Trish unbuckled her seat belt.

"Like I said, it's where we show customers the all-wheel drive. You can drive right over that sandy bit and not get stuck. Drive in reverse if you want."

"I've owned a Subaru," I reminded her.

"No." Trish shook her head. "But I feel magic. Don't you?"

I nodded. Reaching out with my senses, I could feel a hum in the air. A different smell too, like sulfur but sweeter.

"Why'd you *really* bring us here?" I asked.

"Because you're both witches," Lauren said. "This is where I do my potion work. I thought you two might want to see."

"And if we *don't* want to see?" Trish asked her.

"Listen. I'm not trying to lure you to my gingerbread house. We *really* test drive cars here. The dealership owns it. And I *really* do potion work in that building over there. We were just talking about that warning I saw. I thought you two were interested. Ya know, maybe we can figure out if a demon stole my powers."

"We were. I mean, I am," I said.

"That looks like the worst place to do potions I've ever seen," Trish added.

Lauren unbuckled and rolled her eyes. "Well, I haven't taken down my wards yet, have I? Hold on."

She got out of the car and stood beside the open door. Then she muttered something under her breath, waving her hand from side to side like she was Daniel-san waxing on and waxing off.

Suddenly, the partial building was whole again. It was still a bit run down, but nothing like the shell of building we'd originally seen.

"Come on." Lauren waved at us. "Let's get inside, so I can restore the wards. I don't usually do this in the middle of the day."

"Ah, it is the middle of the day," Trish said. "No wonder I'm getting hungry."

"Can't help you there," Lauren said. "I left my last protein bar in my desk at the office."

Before we stepped inside, Trish stopped me, concern on her face. She brushed some purple hair aside. "You're sure you want to go in?"

"I think we can trust Lauren."

"You don't have to trust me if you don't want to," Lauren said. "I understand you've been through an ordeal. It would freak me out. I mean—I am freaked out. If my magic was used like that, then I want to know who took it and why. Honestly, I'm kind of pissed."

"You don't really seem the type of person that gets pissed," Trish said. "Ever. Which is why I'm weirded out by all of this. And you really don't seem the type to have a secret potion-making warehouse."

"Where do you make your potions?"

"Usually the kitchen," Trish said.

Lauren nodded. "I get it. But my mom never brewed a potion at home. She said it was bad luck. And she never wanted my dad to know about us."

"She sounds kind of smart," Trish said.

"Yeah. She was. Just not understanding."

We followed Lauren though the door of the old warehouse. Inside, it was drab and dusty. It was an open concept with almost everything original removed from the inside. A stream of light from a long row of windows lit the center of the room. Smartly, Lauren hadn't removed her sunglasses.

She'd organized that central space with cauldrons of different sizes. One of them emitted steam—the others were empty. To one side of the cauldrons was a podium, and atop it an old book lay open. There were bookcases on the opposite side of the building, none of them the same size or style. Only one of those had books, the rest housed row after row of jars. A few shelves had sealed bags of dried herbs—her ingredients pantry.

In the corner farthest from the door there were *other* things. Things that made sounds. I couldn't make out what was in the cages as they were covered with blankets or sheets.

And on the wall nearest us three large, industrial-size fish tanks like something that might be found at a fish farm gurgled. There were fish in the first one—your guess is as good as mine what kind. In the next were eels. And in the third, turtles and frogs.

"Quite the setup you have here," Trish said in amazement. She looked like a kid in a candy store—not a kid in a gingerbread house.

To me, it was overwhelming. I hadn't grown up knowing I was a witch. I was still getting used to the idea of magic, never mind the peculiar demands of potion-making.

Lauren had been one of the witches who'd gifted me skill in this craft—this was after Kalene, who wasn't good with potions herself, tried to grant me the same gift. This was supposed to ease the burden on Kalene from giving her power away. Now, I realized that Lauren had skill aplenty. Or she was just extremely organized and well supplied.

"I know. I went overboard."

"And then some," Trish said. "I'm guessing you use all parts of the eel, not just the eyes?"

"Oh, definitely. I dry the fins here myself. And the teeth can be used in about anything if you grind them into a powder."

"And the frogs? How many do you—"

"You guys are freaking me out," I interrupted.

"I have almost every ingredient here that any witch could need," Lauren said. "You two are welcome to come by and use a cauldron anytime. I'll teach you the wards."

"That would be—"

"Awesome," Trish finished my sentence. I was going for something more along the lines of nice but no thank you. Trish's trepidation about being here alone with Lauren was forgotten.

"Now, what books are those?" Trish asked her. "Do you know if my mom sold your mom any?"

Lauren shook her head. "I don't think so. Almost all of those have been handed down in my family for generations. I went through some effort to get these though. Like I said, Mom and I had a rift. I'm not even sure I got them all. There's at least one missing. But the one I was talking about—the one Kalene gave me—is on the podium. It's not your everyday potions. They're more specialized."

Trish went to the bookshelf and perused the titles. They were hand-bound books with leather covers. The titles were written on each spine by hand, names like "Love Potions," "For Sickness," and "For Health."

"What kind of potion were you making?" I asked Lauren.

"Oh, you'll think it's silly," Lauren said. "Do I have to tell you?"

"You don't," Trish said. "But now I really want to know."

"Me too."

Trish ran her finger across the spines. Unlike the books in Bewitched Books, these were free of dust.

"In fact," Trish said, "I think we'd really love to look through these—if we could. If you wouldn't mind."

"You're more than welcome." Lauren flipped a few pages in the book on the podium, then pressed the already smoothed page down lovingly. "This was the potion. It's going to sound stupid, but I've been having a rough month with, like everything. First, my mom. Then work. My love life—or lack thereof. I needed *something* to go right. So, I made this potion. It's for luck."

"You can't be serious," Trish gaped.

I rushed over to look at the page. This was exactly what we needed. Well, not exactly. It was what we thought could help us get the *other* book—the one that promised to help me hear my father's words.

"What?" Lauren asked. "Why wouldn't I be serious?"

"'Cause we've been looking for a potion just like this," I said.

I read over the instructions as Trish explained our dilemma.

In blessedly neat handwriting at the top of the page: *A Whole Lotta Luck by Rainbow Moone. 1983.*

It described what the potion did—imbue the drinker luck for an hour or day, depending on how it was stirred. If you stirred it with a demon's finger the effects lasted an entire day.

Then there was the note about the demon and what it could do. But it wasn't really a warning as Lauren had implied. It named a particular demon to use and advised that this demon could steal magic. But to me, it read more like a suggestion.

*For potency, use the demon Beruth. Ask her to stir the mixture with her forefinger. See Demons for Summoning, Binding, and Payment.*

*Be warned: Beruth has been known to steal magic on occasion. And like all demons, she wants her freedom. She cannot be trusted.*

Trish read over my shoulder. "You're sure you didn't summon this demon?"

"I'm not *that* dumb," Lauren said again.

"And this other book— *Demons for Summoning, Binding, and Payment*—do you have it?"

Lauren shook her head. "I guess Kalene might."

"So, did the potion work?" Trish asked.

"Isn't it kind of obvious I haven't taken it yet? It's the one still bubbling in the cauldron."

"Right. Not the luckiest of days when you get accused of murder," I said.

"I've had better." Lauren adjusted her sunglasses. "You know... one way today would be better is if I sold a car..."

"Yeah?"

"And I'm willing to barter. That potion for a sixty-month loan sound okay to you? Or would you rather lease?"

"You mean the potion *and* the car, right?" I had to make sure.

"Twist my arm," Lauren smiled, "and I'll throw in a keychain."

## 21

## WITCHES WITHOUT MOTHERS

The next few hours were spent doing paperwork. *Fun.*

I came away with a new car and a bottle of potion. The name Crookshanks Junior had flitted across my mind. It was too long. And I wasn't about to call a car Junior.

But the slate gray Subaru Outback would never be Crookshanks, no matter how hard it tried. I thought for a second about naming it Grim or Padfoot as Harry had mistaken Sirius's dog form for a bad omen in *Harry Potter and the Prisoner of Azkaban*. That didn't seem right. In the end, I noticed the rack on the roof of the car, and I had my name. Prongs—after Harry's father, James.

Trish called me on my new Bluetooth system—this one was actually built into the stereo system, not aftermarket. I had a backup camera. Who needs mirrors?

"So you have a car," Trish observed over the phone.

"I noticed."

"I'm just saying, my half-a-plan worked out."

"And the potion?"

"That *wasn't* part of my plan. It's why I called. I've been thinking... I don't think you should use it."

"No?"

"I took a picture of the page it was on. We can recreate it."

"Why don't you think I should use Lauren's?"

"Because," Trish said. "I'm still not sure we should trust her. That potion could be anything—getting you to drink it could be what she wanted all along."

"You think?" I shook my head, but Trish couldn't see it. The bug was a few car lengths behind me. The sun was setting over the mountains, casting deep shadows on the trees next to the highway.

"I don't know. Maybe. Why aren't you concerned?"

"For starters," I said, "I'm impervious to poison. If she wanted me dead, I don't think a potion would do it."

"Poison is one thing. Potions are another. You don't know what effect it might have. If it's not the same potion, it could do anything. It could put you to sleep for a year. Change your appearance—and not in a Harry Potter way. There are many things a potion can do that aren't considered poison but would still be awful."

"Okay. I get it."

"But do you, Constance? I can tell you, if anyone knows about harmful potions it's Lauren Whittaker. That operation she has is nuts."

"That's not how you described it a few hours ago," I said.

"Okay. It's impressive. But it's *still* nuts. Why does she need all that? Who's she supplying with potions? That's way more than any witch needs. I still think she could be working with the Faction. That's probably why she was really in D.C."

"My gut says different," I told Trish. "I think we can trust her."

Trish sighed loud enough to be picked up by the receiver. "It's your body. I'm not going to argue if you're determined to put that sludge into it. But please talk to your Gran before you do anything stupid."

"I will," I agreed reluctantly, knowing Gran would try to talk me out of it.

"We'll have to wait till this weekend to try to get the book," Trish said. "I have to work the rest of the week. But in the meantime, Lauren did give me an idea."

"Yeah?"

"You heard what she said in the car—demons can hold a spirit in the shadow realm forever. Sound like anyone we know?"

"Brad," I said.

"That book, *Demons for Summoning, Binding, and Payment*, I think we should try to get our hands on it."

"But Kalene's got it," I told her.

"Yeah, well, she's suspect number two, right?"

"Number one if you ask Gran."

"Right. So, her farmhouse is on the way into town. I'm going to pass you. Follow me there, all right?"

"All right."

∞

KALENE LIVED RIGHT off the highway. A chain-link fence and a small aging house sat close to the road. And surrounding the smaller fence and going on for the next few miles, there was a standard barbed wire fence and a pasture. About a football field's length behind the house, there was a barn that looked more well-kept than the house.

A herd of cattle grazed near a small pond.

The sun was already settled well below the mountains. Its rays crept low, fighting to keep light on the ground.

We pulled onto the concrete drive and hadn't been there long when a shadowy figure appeared at the barn and started our way. Kalene wore a work shirt and jeans with work boots.

She stared at us a minute, squinting with her face twisted in question. And I thought Lauren had played dumb.

"Constance? Trish? What the heck are y'all two doing out here?"

"We came to see you," I said.

She looked even more skeptical. "May I ask why?"

Trish rolled her eyes. "A coven... really?"

"Oh. You heard about that?" Kalene looked away.

"We heard," Trish said. "But I wanted to hear it straight from the horse's mouth."

As if on cue, a horse whinnied in the distance. Kalene smiled a little. "I'm finishing up chores. Y'all walk with me down to the barn. I'll explain."

"Fool me once, shame on me," Trish started. "Fool me twice..."

"Yeah," I agreed. "I don't think we're going to follow you to your barn tonight. We just saw Lauren's whole setup."

"There ain't nothing magic down there," Kalene said. "Just some horses and hay." She looked at me sadly and said, "You saw my magic the other night. You know I can't..."

"You can't what?" Trish asked.

She looked away.

"I think I know what she means," I said. "Her magic is fading."

"Fading? Fading like how?"

"Like every time I use it," Kalene said, "I think it might be the last."

Trish frowned. "I'm still not following."

Tears began to well up in Kalene's eyes. "Come on, Trish. You've known for a while. Think about it. It's basically like the magic skipped a generation. I don't even have a familiar. When I turned forty, one never showed up. And the little magic I do have, I use to keep this farm running.

"The reason I want a coven is because I want to see magic again. To see it like I did when I was little—when my mom was alive and powerful."

"Is that why you gave Lauren that book? To see her be powerful?"

"It's a reason." She nodded.

"What's the other?" I asked.

She looked away again, and this time a tear did stream down her cheek. "I can't read them anymore. None of the books. The words have no meaning. You might as well take them," she told Trish.

It was like that girl Merritt, only in reverse. Kalene had a connection with magic through her mother. So why were her powers waning?

"I'll take one book," Trish said. "Because it's part of the reason we're here. And I'm borrowing it. If it's truly as bad as you say, then there has to be a reason your magic is fading. Kalene, I'm sorry. I didn't know."

"Yeah, well, we all have our problems." She wiped her tears away with the sleeve of her stained work shirt.

Her words rang true.

Trish had lost her mother in one of the worst ways—her father had killed her mother for magic. I had lost my mother because of magic. She was just gone one day and never came back. And Kalene had lost her mother in a fire.

"Kalene," I said. "What do you remember about when your mother died?"

"Not much." She inhaled. "She'd been distant for years. She hardly used her magic anymore. I thought maybe it was something I'd done. I thought she was mad at me."

"And the fire killed her?"

She nodded. "Maybe her magic failed too. Maybe it's *our* curse. Our family curse. And she just never told me."

The three of us stood there a minute longer, and it wasn't long before tears streamed down my face. Even Trish had one threatening her black eyeliner.

∼

I DROVE HOME with the radio off, alone with my thoughts. Maybe Trish was right. Maybe I shouldn't trust Lauren. Maybe I shouldn't trust Kalene. One of them had to be lying. And I needed to dig for the truth. It was out there somewhere.

I stopped in Gran's driveway and thought on it more. Maybe it was all a setup. Maybe neither of them had anything to do with my dad's death.

I got out, but before I could get to Gran's door, Trish's yellow bug stopped in the road. She rolled her window down and handed me the book that Kalene had given her.

"It should be good for some light reading," she said. "You available Friday for a trip down to Virginia Beach? We can scope things out then figure out our plan of attack."

"I thought you didn't want me to take the potion?"

"I'll have one made by Friday. So, are you down? You're driving, by the way. That's the rule when you get a new car."

"I can't on Friday," I said. "I already have plans."

"With?"

"Dave—well, his girls. We're having a sleepover. You're invited if you'd like to come."

"You know," Trish said, "I think I'm going to pass. What about Saturday morning after Dave makes you his famous pancakes or whatever? Sound good?"

"I'll have to ask my boss for the day off."

"Oh, I know how your boss can be. She's kind of a B, ya know? That word that rhymes with witch?"

"I know the word."

"I think one Saturday won't hurt. Read this demon book and report back."

"Will do," I said.

Trish was right about a lot of things.

Gran didn't think it was a good idea to take the potion. Also, she tested the new car for spells, which only gave me the idea to try and make it fly one day. I'm an Arthur Weasley at heart.

And in my reading of the book, I found three contenders —demons that might have Brad. I showed Gran. The question was, did we really want to summon one?

## 22

## IN WITCH I HEAR A FAMILIAR VOICE

The next day, Gran was up early, bustling around downstairs. The garage door opened. The Buick's engine started. The garage door closed again.

Mornings without Gran were few and far between. She was a homebody. I served as her grocery and general delivery person. The kind delivery drivers and mailman performed her other essential tasks.

Gran preferred not to dine out. She didn't attend a book club or play bridge. She watched TV and worked magic spells. The only time she left was to get her hair done or to do magic in the graveyard.

It was too early for either.

I knew Stevie's schedule well enough to know that he'd already returned from the shadow realm and would be asleep on a cushion somewhere until noon. We were excited to tell him the good news—that we'd found a possible avenue to find Brad.

But that could wait. The prospect of a lazy morning by myself brightened my spirits. I traipsed downstairs in my night shirt and poured a cup of coffee. I was bent over and halfway inside the refrigerator looking for the creamer with my backside on display when the backdoor flew open.

What I should've done was straighten up and turn around, removing my derrière from view. What I did was look over my shoulder at the door to see who it was.

Eyes wide, Hilda Jeffries came to an abrupt stop on the threshold.

She only gaped at me for a second before Gran ran into her from behind and sent her tumbling—right into my backside.

I went sprawling.

Hilda was smarter. She used her magic to stop in midair, then without moving a muscle, straightened. Her posture was perfect. "Well, that was unpleasant."

"Curses and cauldrons, Constance." She learned that from Trish. "What in the devil are you doing?"

"I was, uh, looking for the creamer," I said.

"We're out. Looks like someone needs to go to the grocery store today."

*I.e. me.*

"Okay." I rolled my eyes. "Now, what are y'all doing? I thought you left."

Gran shook her head. "I moved the car. Didn't you say we needed to call one of those demons?"

"What does the car have to do with that? And Hilda," I said, "it's nice to see you. I only wish I'd known we were having company."

"Cute panties." Hilda smiled.

"You said we had to call a demon," Gran repeated. "So, I called the expert. And I moved the car because my casting circle is in the garage."

"Oh." I was having trouble functioning. Without the magic of coffee, my brain couldn't catch up. "I thought maybe we'd wait for Trish. And you said summoning demons was dangerous and we shouldn't do it."

"I told you not to do it without me," Gran corrected. "And I said it was a bad practice—one Hilda here is familiar with. It's why I called her last night."

"Terrible practice," Hilda said. "I knew a witch once who fumbled her circle. She had demon lodged in her head for weeks. And she was lucky, it was a lesser demon. Otherwise, I don't think we'd have gotten it out."

"Are you sure we should do this?" I asked.

"I got us the expert," Gran said.

"Rainbow was the expert," Hilda countered. "But I'm happy to help. And I told Jez that I wake up early every morning to do my Rock Body workouts and I'd be over right after. I'm guessing that message never made it to *your* ears."

"Good guess."

"I might've forgotten to tell her," Gran acknowledged. "Forgive an old lady this once. But I can't say it won't happen again. The mind isn't what it used to be."

"It's just another muscle," Hilda said. "You've gotta work it like I do these." She flexed. It reminded me that I hadn't been on a run or done yoga in forever. I'd been focusing on other things—magic, Brad, my dad's murder. I'd put myself on the back burner.

Gran scowled. "I think I sweated enough with Richard Simmons to last me the rest of my days."

"I'm sure you did." Hilda laughed. "Now, are we ready to start?"

"I'm gonna maybe put on some clothes," I said. "And where's Stevie? I was looking for him."

"Stevie and Herby are in the shadow realm. They're looking in on us, from there to here. You see, they see us in shadow. Hence the name." Herbie was her familiar.

"Right." I knew that much.

"When we summon the demon—and bind him—they bind him from there as well. Call it an extra layer of protection. Demons are all sorts of tricky. We have to be prepared."

"And which of these demons we should call?" Gran pointed at the book, open on the table.

"I think this one." Hilda tapped the page. "But it could be this one or this one. There's only so many operating these days. Lucky for us they don't multiply like the werewolves do."

"Hey!"

"I know," she said. "There are a few good ones. But still, just the thought of one." She shuddered. "Gives me the heebie-jeebies, ya know."

"Why?"

"Have you ever been on the wrong side of a werewolf? They don't think clearly during the full moon. Does the same thing to kids. You know, I was a third-grade teacher before I retired."

"I didn't," I said.

"All right. Enough history lessons." Gran had her finger on the page. She took a deep breath and chanted,

"Eeny, meeny, slithering snail.
Catch a demon by its tail.
If he hollers a screeching gale,
Make sure your fingers do not fail.
My Aunt Margaret told me to pick the best one.
And you are *it*."

"THERE, it's this one, Custos the Conniving." She read off what was needed for his summoning. "Now, get your clothes on, girl."

A few minutes later, I met them in the garage. Gran was pouring salt. She made a circle outside another circle—one I didn't remember seeing before, probably because Gran's car was usually parked on top of it.

This circle was made of what looked to be silver and embedded in the cement. Inside was a hexagram. A circle inside the hexagram held a pentagram. And each triangular point of the hexagram outside the inner pentagram had runes of its own, in the same silver. The larger circle was around five feet wide. The salt circle Gran had made was wider still.

"Salt's good in a pinch." Hilda winked.

I smiled.

"It's a pun. Get it?"

"Not funny the first time," Gran said, "and not funny the second. I told you she wouldn't laugh."

"Why do we need so many circles?" I asked them.

"Extra layers of protection," Hilda answered.

I gestured toward the circle. "And how did I not know this was here?"

"That's because you're about as observant as five-year-old," Gran huffed. She put a bottle of Creel Creek Vineyard wine inside the circle along with a gallon of Rocky Road ice cream and a plastic spoon.

"Now, stand right there." She positioned me. "We need to make an equilateral triangle."

Who knew being a witch required so much geometry? We used the shapes on the floor as a guide. Then Gran nodded to Hilda, and we were ready.

Hilda intoned,

"Let my voice be heard in the depths so deep,"
"Let the words penetrate the nether worlds and the Never Nether.
Through the shadow realm and into the pit of despair known to all as hell.
I call to the jailer of spirits.
To the demon guard.
I call to Custos the Conniving.
And by the laws of our ancient craft, I bind thee to this circle.
I call, and I bind thee, so that we may seek answers to questions not yet formed.
I call."

Black smoke filled the room. I accidentally breathed some and almost went into a coughing fit. But despite the garage door being down and having no other ventilation, the smoke dissipated into wisps, revealing a man standing as cool as a cucumber in the center of the circle.

Not a man. Not really. He had on a black suit and tie and dark sunglasses. It made him look like one of the Men in Black or a wannabe David Duchovny.

He removed the glasses to reveal crimson eyes. Then he folded them, tucked them into his breast pocket, and looked down.

"This is what you call payment?" His teeth were a shade too white and his canines a tad too sharp.

"It was our understanding that demons crave something cold," Hilda said as the demon reached for the ice cream. He pulled it open and dug in. His tongue, the tip of which forked slightly, licked the plastic spoon until it was bare, then he went in for another scoop.

"Tis true," he said. "But let's stick with the classics next time. Chocolate or vanilla. My ice cream doesn't need marshmallows or these hard bits."

"Noted."

"And this is the best alcohol you could find?"

"It's good," I said meekly.

"Maybe," the demon replied. "But it's lacking in potency, isn't it?"

"I have some rum under the sink," Gran offered.

The demon actually hissed this time. Not just his words. Mostly with his tongue, I think. "I'll sssssssstick with the wine."

He used a sharp fingernail to pry the cork out, then his too-sharp teeth to wrench it free. He spat it toward me, but the circle held. It bounced back toward him.

"A *solid* circle. You three know your stuff." He looked from me to Gran to Hilda, then around to me again and said, "Or two of you do. To what do I owe the pleasure?"

"We believe you're incarcerating someone, and we need him back," I told the demon.

"That doesn't sound much like a question." He took a pained swig of wine. "Really, ladies. You're wasting my time. I do have a dungeon to run."

"And what type of spirits do you hold in this dungeon?" Gran asked him.

"Finally! A question. I hold all manner of spirits in my dungeon. Mortal spirits. The Fae—if they've been naughty. Some demons. Some angels even. The cost of battle is high."

"What about familiars?" I asked.

"You mean the Fallen?"

"Aren't demons also Fallen?"

"Well," he smirked, "we fell, if that's what you mean. But it was more on purpose. These beings you speak of are rather aimless, are they not?"

"That's your opinion," Hilda told him. "They're rather useful to us."

"Yes, well, that *is* the problem. We all serve a master of some sort. And to answer your question, I do have some of the Fallen within my realm."

"Your prison," Gran spat.

"Tomayto, tomahto. I picked that one up from one of yours. Does this familiar you're looking for have a name?"

"Brad," I said.

"That is a silly mortal name. I mean his *real* name."

I tried to remember the metallic shrieking growl Brad told me was his name when he'd first appeared. It sounded like a train crash—there was just no way I could remember it.

"Oh?" Custos, the demon, looked thoughtful. "Are those your familiars in the shadow realm? How good of them to show up. You're lucky they know how to speak Ancient. Yes, I do remember that name. He's only been with me a short while. Much shorter than his sentence."

"His sentence?" Gran and I asked in unison.

The demon shrugged. "Whatever you want to call what I do. I made a deal. I will hold this Brad, as you call him, for the next hundred earth years."

"Who was this deal with? A warlock?" Gran asked.

"I cannot disclose my clients. But no. No warlock can strike a deal like that with me. Someone else."

There was no time to think about that. "How can I get him back?" I asked.

"Another *good* question. You can't." He swallowed the dregs of his wine. "Is that all you needed?"

"What do you mean she can't?" Hilda asked for me.

"As I said, I require payment for what I do—or don't do, in this case. And nothing you have here will suffice. Thanks for the Rocky Road." He rolled his crimson eyes.

He was so condescending. In that regard, he reminded me of Stevie. Brad had never been that way. Neither was Twinkie, for that matter.

"One more question," I pleaded. "Can I hear his voice?"

"I don't know? Can you?"

I huffed. "May I hear his voice?"

"Better." He set the wine bottle down next to the spent carton of ice cream. Then he raised both hands, closed his eyes, and drew a deep breath.

"Hello?" The familiar booming of Brad's voice echoed through the garage as if it was shouted into a tunnel.

"Brad!" I yelled.

The demon waggled a finger to me. "You didn't ask me to allow him to hear you."

With all the emotion I could muster, I reached out with my magic, attempting to bridge the distance between us. "Brad!" I yelled again. "Brad! Can you hear me?"

"Is someone there?" Brad asked. "I can feel a presence. Constance? Is that you?"

The demon's red eyes went wide. He put his arms down in a sweeping motion. "I don't know how you did that, girl. But you, my dear, are bad for business." He leveled his gaze at Gran then Hilda, then back to me. "And should any of you ever contact me again, I'll require *real* payment."

"But what—"

"Fffffffigure it out," he hissed. "I'll keep your familiar company until then."

With another puff of smoke, he vanished. When he was gone, it felt like all the magic was gone from the room. I was drained. I couldn't perform another spell that day. Or the next.

With my magical reserves depleted, I almost felt like the under-forty me. The problem was, I never wanted to feel that powerless again.

I realized that I *liked* being a witch. I liked using magic. And it was time I saved Brad.

If I could only figure out how.

## 23

## IN WITCH I SLEEPOVER

Friday came too fast. I felt antsy. This wasn't a date. It was something worse. A test. These girls meant everything to Dave, and them liking me meant everything to me.

I got to his house around seven. It was a nice house as houses go, but nothing too remarkable. The outside was well kept, the lawn mowed, and there was a two-car garage, one side filled with things like a tool chest and every saw known to mankind. The stairs to the second floor started in the foyer. The inside was clean and mostly tidy—except for the girls' rooms, which they had to show me.

Dave had ordered pizza. The girls ate and guzzled Coke like a JV football team. They weren't shy around me, and I liked that.

We watched a movie together. Dave snuck his hand into mine until the youngest, Kacie, climbed on his lap.

Elsie cuddled up on the couch beside him. A little standoffish, Allie, the oldest, sat on a chair on the other side of the room.

They shared Dave's features. His thin lips. Allie had his

nose. Their hair wasn't quite as dark. Kacie's light brown could've been mistaken for blonde in certain light. And Elsie barely had any hair. It was cropped around her oval face, which I learned wasn't by choice. It was due to an incident with gum.

I shared my own hair troubles with them, scooting the wig back to reveal the hair now coming in. Elsie's gap-toothed grin helped keep the others' laughter from hurting my feelings too much. And her hand kept going to her mouth, wiggling yet another loose tooth. Thankfully, I had found a dentist to repair my tooth.

During the movie, Allie kept asking me questions like where I was from? California. Where I went to school? UCLA. Where I'd worked before I moved here? At a few tech companies.

"I heard you're a witch, is that *true*?" she finally asked.

I nodded.

"How does magic work anyway? Can you show us?"

I was still depleted from using my magic to reach out to Brad.

"I'm still learning," I said. "Not tonight. Maybe I can show you some other time."

They agreed that was a great idea and thought the next time we went to the park I should put on a show.

"It's not *that* kind of magic," I tried to tell them.

"Just one trick tonight," Kacie pleaded. "Please. Please."

How could I say no to that face?

"Just one. And that's it. Promise?"

"We promise!"

Overwhelmed, I wanted to turn to Dave for help, but he'd excused himself to the kitchen, standing over a pizza box with a bottle of beer.

"Come on, you two," Allie said. "Give her a break."

"Thank you." I smiled at her.

"Seriously," she said, "they're impressed when dad pretends to yank off his thumb. You could try something small."

*Something small*, I thought, not sure what to do—if anything. I was being peer pressured by not-even-tweens.

"Can you make my doll come alive?" Kacie asked.

*Definitely not.*

"That'd be creepy." Allie shook her head.

I agreed. "What if I light that candle on the mantle?"

"Mom loved that smell," Allie said, not so enthused.

"Oh, well, I don't have to—"

"No! Light the candle." Elsie clapped.

I looked to Allie for approval. And she nodded.

"All right."

I tried to formulate a simple rhyme. A simple rhyme for simple magic.

"Let it flicker. Let it burn.
It's a scent that we yearn… to—"

I sighed. "That wasn't very good. Let me try again."

"They put you on the spot, did they?" Dave poked his head in.

"Just a little," I admitted.

"Dad! No boys allowed anymore."

"All right, Kacie. I thought you might want a kiss goodnight."

*If she didn't, I'd take one.*

"Oh! I do. I do."

"Me too!" Elsie screamed.

Dave moseyed over, his nearly empty beer bottle in hand, and doled out kisses. I didn't get one. And I was a little jealous because of it.

"Okay," he said, "let's see this magic, then I'll go."

"Fine."

I drew a breath.

> "Just a light to give us sight.
> Let it glow til someone blows."

THE CANDLE SPUTTERED INTO FLAME. I sighed with relief. Somehow doing magic for Dave's little girls was just as hard as doing it to save my life. *Ugh.*

"Y'all have a good night," he said smiling. Then he whispered in my ear, "I'll be up late if you want to come upstairs." Then to the room, he said, "They usually go down by nine or nine thirty—since it's not a school night. Ten's the limit. Don't let them tell you otherwise."

They tried to tell me otherwise.

Kacie passed out near the end of the second movie, *The Princess Bride*. My pick. Afterward, Allie lay down on a pallet on the floor—they'd kindly given me the couch—her dark hair spread out around her. Within minutes, soft snoring erupted.

But at ten o'clock, Elsie really came out of her shell. She talked and talked and talked some more. She got her stuffed animals from her room. She called them her lovies and told me their names and where they were born and everything I could've wanted to know about them—and then some.

She told me that she thinks her dad likes me and that she likes me... and that Allie and Kacie like me too.

She told me that she had the best mommy ever, and that she missed her. Then she asked why my eyes had tears in them and if I *boo boo*. "Do you need a Band-Aid?"

Later, in the middle of a sentence, she nodded off.

I pulled the blanket around her and waited a minute to make sure she was really asleep. Then I slipped off the couch, blew out the candle, and headed for the stairs.

Dave's door was cracked open. The lamp was on and the Agatha Christie book had dropped on his chest. He was passed out just like his three girls downstairs. I knew he'd probably be mad, but I decided *not* to wake him.

He looked so peaceful. How could Hilda think there was anything threatening about a werewolf?

Gently—just like Buttercup kissing Westley—I kissed him on the cheek.

I turned off his lamp. Downstairs, I cozied up on the chair. In what seemed like no time, the girls were awake with the TV blaring. And Dave was in the kitchen making coffee and flipping pancakes.

## 24

## IN WITCH WE GET LUCKY

A couple of hours later, after breakfast and Saturday morning cartoons, I left to meet Trish at Bewitched Books.

*Those girls*, I thought. *They're so cute.* Which only made things harder.

Dave was sweet and also cute. Actually, now that he'd shaved his ridiculous mustache, he bordered more on the hawt side, spelled H-A-W-T.

*Curses and cauldrons.*

I sighed, ruminating what I *should've* done when I went up to Dave's room. But our relationship was still fresh. I wasn't even sure if I could call it a relationship exactly.

Calling him my boyfriend was out of the question. Part of me wanted to. I mean, I'd gotten the okay from Elsie— what more did I need? Well, aside from him asking me, nothing.

It was like Cyrus said, Dave had and would always have a lot on his plate. He'd probably drag his feet on this for months, if not years. It was time we talked. *Really* talked about what the future held... if anything.

Trish's canary yellow bug was angle parked in front of the store. I got out, but Trish met me at the door. She had a satchel around her chest in her trademark color. She turned the placard to CLOSED and locked the door.

"I've just got to finish this spell." She held up a finger. "One second."

She whipped out her phone with one hand and began to mutter. With the finger she'd pointed at me, she traced the outside of the door where her wards—her magical protections of the store—were most potent.

She'd told me about them once. Gran had something similar on her house, something that kept evil away. It had worked on the warlock.

But the problem with a storefront is you have to allow people to enter—almost always unannounced. Thus, most wards were useless—especially when the door's unlocked and that OPEN placard is visible.

The best Trish could do was something like this. She put traces on everyone who entered and smaller spells to protect against burglary or theft. I say smaller, but those awful department store tags with ink cartridges had nothing on them. Steal a book from Bewitched Books and be *hexed* in consequence.

"And done," Trish said. She held up her phone. The map application was giving directions in a snotty tone. "I took a page from your book."

"That wasn't on purpose." To find Nell Baker's cabin in the woods, I'd tried a spell, and the magic had decided the best way to convey directions was with an app like this one.

"A happy accident. We're lucky maps are so closely tied with the Earth." Trish looked down at the phone. "Hmm. I thought she lived in Virginia Beach?"

"That's what she said," I said but without Michael Scott's gusto.

"Then why do these directions lead west?"

I shrugged. "I guess we'll have to see. It doesn't show you the final destination, does it?"

She shook her head. "No, it's turn by turn. Your guess is as good as mine."

We got in the new car and headed west down Main Street, passing the burned shell of courthouse.

"What's even out this way?" I asked her.

"The mountains. The lake."

"We have a lake?"

I could almost hear Trish roll her eyes. "When you move somewhere, Constance, you really should get out and explore it. At least a little. Out this way is where Creel Creek gets kinda beautiful."

"It does?"

"Well, not the town, obviously. But the outdoors—they do. And FYI, I live out this way."

"I've never been to your house," I said. "Is that weird?"

"It's an apartment. And it's not much to look at. Trust me, I'm not offended. Hell, Twinkie doesn't even live there. That should tell you something."

It was true, Trish's familiar lived in the shop and hardly ever left it. When she did, it was to go to the shadow realm, which she and Stevie no longer had to do. We knew where to find Brad, just not how to get him out.

The computer voice told us to take the next turn down a country road.

"Okay. I think I know where we're going. It's close to the lake."

"Where?"

"Have you ever heard of the Creel Creek Mountain

Lodge?"

"Yeah." I tried to remember where. My eyes went wide. "That's where Jade—Ivana—saw a ghost. They sponsored an episode of *Creel Creek After Dark*."

Again, I could tell Trish rolled her eyes. "They would," she said. "The owners are a bit out there. They're shifters of some kind, I forget which. They're the type that want paranormals and mortals to live in harmony. Good luck."

"What's so wrong with that?" To me, it sounded better than it was now. I hated keeping everything a secret.

"You remember how everyone reacted at the Midsummer Festival?" Trish asked. "Imagine that on a larger scale. Seriously, it's best we stay hidden."

"Yeah." I sighed. "I just think it'd be easier not to hide who we are."

"Well, you do it better than anyone else I know."

"I'm not sure if that's a compliment or not."

"It's a half compliment," Trish said. "Think about it. If we were in a lineup, I'd be identified as the potential witch. You'd be singled out like that show on MTV back in the day."

"Hardee har har."

"What? I kinda liked it."

"Me too," I admitted.

The navigation told us to turn again after the sign—*Creel Creek Mountain Lodge*. The long driveway followed the edge of a golf course to a resort style building reminiscent of an oversized hunting cabin—brown timbers with a green roof. It looked like it was built from a giant set of Lincoln Logs.

I parked in the first available spot. A sign pointed to the country club entrance; the lobby was straight ahead.

I didn't stop the engine.

"Is this it?" I asked.

"Room 211," the navigation voice said.

"I guess so." Trish shrugged.

"So what now? Should we wait for her to come outside or something?"

"This blows," Trish huffed. "It's not like we had a good plan going into it, but I thought we had a few hours' drive to think of one. I can't believe she's still here in Creel Creek."

"Neither can I," I said. "Maybe we just take the lucky potion and let it do its magic."

"That's one thought."

"You have a better idea?"

"No."

Trish rummaged in her bag and brought out two bottles. She brushed purple and midnight hair out of her face and eyed them. "Listen. I know you said you wanted to use Lauren's potion, but I hoped you'd reconsider. I made two."

I dug out the bottle Lauren had given me. While the clear bottles weren't identical, the contents looked much the same. They both held greenish-brown liquid the consistency of glue. Trish had corked hers. Lauren's had a cap because of course her giant warehouse potion factory had a bottling component.

"They look the same," I stated the obvious.

"Most potions do," Trish said. "It's just what happens when you combine elements that should never be ingested by a mortal and simmer them over a fire."

"Fair enough. But I still think we can trust Lauren."

Trish eyed me skeptically. "Is this really about trust or something else?"

"I'm not following."

She shook her head. "I can't believe it. And you said I was impressed by her setup? I know what this is about. You think she's a better potion maker than me."

"I didn't say that."

"You didn't have to. It's written all over your face."

"I'm sorry. I—"

"No. You're right. I'm not fancy like her. I don't have a bottling line. But I know my stuff. Your Gran's asked me for help before."

"Trish I—"

"I get it," Trish spat. "Your gut says Lauren's okay. But can't we also trust mine? Can't you trust me to make a decent potion?"

"I trust you."

"Then drink up." Trish handed me her second bottle

"You really think this is going to make us lucky?"

"If it doesn't, you can take the other one tomorrow."

"Fine."

She smothered a smile.

"You said all that just to make me drink *your* potion, didn't you?"

"I don't know what you're talking about."

"You know I trust you—your magic skills, your potion making skills, and your judgment. You just said all that to make me drink this."

"Believe what you want to believe, Constance." She sighed, exasperated, despite getting her way. "Bottoms up." Trish yanked the cork from the bottle with her teeth.

I struggled to do the same with mine.

We clinked bottles and drank the potion.

Trish was right, no one was going to pick me out in a witch lineup. But the usual suspects would be there—her, Gran, Agatha. Even Hilda and Kalene.

Then I realized why I trusted Lauren—because she was like me. We could both pass for normal in this paranormal world.

## 25
## THE CREEL CREEK MOUNTAIN LODGE

There was no concierge at the Creel Creek Mountain Lodge. In fact, there wasn't a soul in the lobby. Decked out with hunting trophies, leather chairs and couches, the centerpiece of the room was an unlit fireplace. To the side, out of the way, was the receptionist desk with no receptionist. A bell was placed prominently on the counter. I imagined its daily use equaled roughly the number of guests each night.

Having been here before, Trish paid no attention to any of it. "Room 211," she repeated over and over until we reached the elevator.

"How are we going to explain how we found her?"

"Good question. We'll have to figure it out." Trish hit the button for the second floor. There were only two. "Are you feeling any luckier?"

"No. You?"

"Not really. I wonder if I didn't add enough frog spleen. I'm running low, so I skimped a little."

My stomach lurched. It's one thing to see the list of

ingredients in a potion and a whole other to think about them when they're sitting at the bottom of your stomach.

When the doors slid open on the second floor, I began to feel different. A little lighter on my feet. A little excited. My hands tingled the way they do when my magic reaches to me.

"Do you feel that?" Trish basically skipped down the hall.

Trish... skipped.

I knew I felt different but not *that* different. What did this potion do to her?

"I guess it's working." I hurried down the hall to catch up.

At room 211, Trish knocked straight away without saying anything to me.

"Trish!" I hissed.

And she smiled. She actually smiled without saying anything snarky first.

"Just a sec," said a woman's voice on the other side of the door.

A minute later the young woman from the store undid the lock and the chain then opened the door a crack. The same pretty young face greeted us. Her dirty blonde hair was pulled into a messy bun. She'd done her eye makeup—wings—but nothing else.

"Really? You?" She glowered at me, then she sized Trish up.

I froze. The potion *hadn't* worked. Trish must've made a mistake. *Stupid frog spleen.* I wanted to bolt.

But the door opened wide. She ushered us inside like it was nothing.

"You're early," she said. "I thought you said noon in your email?"

"Sorry... is this okay?" Trish rolled with it. "We could come back at, uh, noon."

"Nah, it's fine. I don't have anywhere I need to be anyway." She shrugged.

"That's good." Trish smiled again.

The door closed behind me, and the three of us were awkwardly close together in a small room that looked like every hotel I'd ever stayed in.

"One of you can sit at the desk." She indicated the desk. "And one on the end of the bed. That's not the one I sleep in, so no worries there."

"Sounds good." Trish took the desk, which left me the edge of the hard mattress.

"So, like I said in the email, I'm Merritt. Let me guess who you are." She pointed to Trish. "You're Athena. And you're Ivana."

"Spot on." Trish grinned at me.

*Yes, I get it*, I thought. She thinks we're from the podcast.

"I knew it!" Merritt turned to me. "You know, no offense, but you always sound kinda stuffy on the show. Straight-laced. Then again, I guess you do work in that unorthodox bookshop, so I shouldn't be too surprised to see you here."

"Is that why you stayed?" I asked her. "For this, I mean—to talk to us? It's been a little while since you were in the shop."

"It's one reason." She took a seat on the other bed. "It's been kind of a crazy few weeks. But you don't want to hear about any of that."

"Sure we do," Trish said.

Merritt frowned.

Trish waved her off. "Oh, no worries. It's off the record. We'd just like to get to know more about you before..."

"Before I show you the book... Right... Well, you've seen

it, haven't you? It's funny, you know—the way you responded to the email, I didn't expect this. It was like you'd never seen a book like it before. And now I know you see them every day." She sighed. "It's pretty silly. I hope I'm not wasting your time."

"You're not," Trish said.

"Definitely not," I agreed. "Now, what's been going on aside from your grandmother passing away?"

"Right. I told you I was raised by my uncle and aunt. And they're awesome people. They are. But ever since this whole thing with my grandmother, they've been concerned for me. They told me some things about my *real* mom—things they thought I should know."

"Like?"

"Like she's into Wicca. That's not what you say, is it? She's a Wiccan. She believes in witchcraft—like *really* believes."

"Do you know where your mom is now?"

"No. I tried to find her once. I'm sure my grandmother could've put us in touch. Maybe I should call her lawyer?"

"That'd be a good idea," I agreed.

Merritt sighed. "When I went to your bookstore, well, it seemed like the kind of place she might like. I had this feeling like maybe she's even been there before."

"It's possible," Trish said. "I could find out for you. I should probably tell you that I own Bewitched Books. It was my mother's shop."

"I just work there." I raised a hand.

"You keep it running," Trish countered.

"Cool." Merritt continued, "Anyway, my grandmother didn't say anything about Wicca—or I don't remember it. Her lawyer just gave me the book."

"Right."

"Okay." Trish nodded encouragingly.

"I was only going to stay here one night. I came here right after the bookstore, and when I got here, there was this flyer. It was for *your* podcast. I listened to it. I listened to every episode. I have to say, I think I'm a believer.

"And this week, when you talked about those witches in the graveyard. Well, I think I might be one. You know what I mean—I wasn't with them or anything. But I think I'm a witch.

"And the funny thing is, as soon as I started thinking that, I started being able to make sense of some of the stuff in my book."

Trish's eyes went wide.

"I thought I could show you," Merritt said. "Then you'd have definitive proof that witches exist. Or something like that. But now I just feel silly."

"Why?" I asked her.

"Because... because you have books like mine. I saw them. And I guess you know Wiccans exist. Or whatever. It's just weird how I couldn't read it until now. So, I guess the book's not evidence of anything then, is it?"

"It *is* evidence," Trish said. "And I'm glad we got here first."

Merritt cocked her head to the side. "What do you mean?"

"Merritt, we're not really the hosts of *Creel Creek After Dark*."

"You're not? But I—"

"Oh, I'm sure they'll be here soon. Listen. I'm going to tell you something, and I don't think it's going to come as much of a shock to you... Witches are real. You're a witch. I'm a witch. Constance there, she's a witch too."

"But—"

"The hosts of that podcast wouldn't know it if a real witch stood in front of them and said *hocus pocus*."

"I knew it," Merritt exclaimed. "I knew something was going on in this town. Real witches. And by real, you mean like *real* magic. You weren't just like, pretending in that graveyard, were you?"

"It's real." With the swipe of her finger and a muttered word, Trish spelled the curtains open and sunlight flooded the room.

Merritt barely acknowledged it. She kept saying, "I knew it. I knew it. Real werewolves. And real ghosts. Did y'all know, this place is haunted?"

Trish shrugged noncommittally.

"I'm sorry. I'm just freaking out. I *freaking* knew it."

"Why are you so sure about the werewolf thing?" I had to ask.

"I'm just am. I can feel it in my gut." She stood up and paced. "Wait... so, if you're not Athena and Ivana or whoever, then why *did* you come here?"

"It's going to sound worse than it is," Trish admitted.

"You're came here to take my book."

Trish shook her head, then she was standing too, pleading our case. "It's not like that. Think of the shop as a layaway program. Books always find their true owners in the end. But you won't become a witch for a while."

"Why not? I can read the book now. How long does it take?"

"You won't get powers until you're forty."

"Forty?" Her jaw dropped and she turned to me. "Is that why you asked how old I was?"

I nodded.

"Eighteen years. Are you serious? I have to wait eighteen years until I can do magic?"

"I thought you said you were about to turn twenty-nine."

"Yeah, well, I lied. It seemed like you wanted me to be older. I can't believe this. I have to wait eighteen years before I can use the book?" She leaned her head back and let out a huge sigh.

"It could have been worse," Trish chimed in. "When we came here, we thought you'd never be able to do magic. We thought you'd never become a witch."

"Why not?"

"Because of your connection to your mother. Or lack thereof."

"So how can you be sure I *will* become a witch? If you take my book, then isn't that like taking my magic away?"

"It's not," Trish said. "You're bound to that book now. You'll get it back. I promise you that. But it can only be used by a practitioner. And for eighteen more years, that's not you."

"This so figures. I know saying this always happens to me is cliché but it's *so* true. This kind of stuff *always* happens to me."

"It sounds like it," I said.

She sighed, then performed a back flop onto her bed. "I don't know what to do. I believe you. But I told those other two about the book. They'll be expecting to see it. And they seem really nice."

"They're okay," Trish lied. "And honestly, you could show them the book. They'd have the same trouble reading and comprehending it as you."

"But they'd know something is up." Merritt sat up.

"That is a problem," I said.

She turned to face me. "I'm sorry about the other day. I really am. Now, I have this feeling that you two should take the book. I'll make something up. I'll tell them I lost it."

"You're sure?" Trish asked her.

She went to the niche that served as a closet, then bent down and unlocked the safe. She fished out the book. "I can't explain it, but I trust you two. And now I know I'll be a witch. One day."

"You will," Trish agreed.

"Is it all right if we keep in contact? Are you two on social media?"

Trish smiled and nodded.

The potion had worked. Not only had we felt lucky—but even when we'd bungled things, they'd been corrected somehow. *Oh, right, by magic*, I thought.

We said our goodbyes and left with the book in hand. I was beginning to feel the magic fading away.

We took the stairs down and were just passing the elevator when I saw a familiar face glaring at me. Jade's eyes went wide. She reached her hand out to stop the doors, but it was too late. The elevator dinged. There was a loud hum as it inched upward.

"That was lucky," Trish said.

"Or not."

I had the sinking feeling that taking this book would come back to bite us.

## 26

## CREEL CREEK AFTER DARK EPISODE 55

It's getting late.
Very late.
*The creeping dread of tomorrow haunts your dreams.*
*It's dark out. Are you afraid?*
*Welcome to Creel Creek After Dark.*

**A**thena: I'm your host, Athena Hunter.
**Ivana:** And I'm Ivana Steak.
**Athena:** This is episode fifty-five. And we're happy to be interviewing our first guest in some time.

**Ivana:** That's right. Our special guest today is a new listener of the program—one who believes she has a connection to the paranormal community. She contacted us after the last episode, which you'll recall, was about our local group of witches.

**Athena:** It's called a coven, Ivana.

**Ivana:** Right you are, Athena. Although we can't be sure that this coven was truly a coven.

**Athena:** Not until today. Our guest, we're going to meet her this afternoon, actually believes that she might be a witch. And she's going to open up about her life and show us what she believes is proof that the witches here in Creel Creek do exist.

**Ivana:** We know they exist, Athena. We just don't know if they're witches.

**Athena:** You know what I mean. Anyway, we're off to our favorite local hotel, The Creel Creek Mountain Lodge, to meet her. So, stick around, we'll be back after this message from today's sponsor.

**Woman's voice:** Are you low on energy? Are you feeling sick? Tired? Or maybe you just need some good fortune to turn things around. Enhancing Elixirs are potent pick-me-ups with a punch. Never mind the taste, it's the effects you're after. Order your first half dozen vials now and receive lucky number seven on the house.

**Woman's voice:** Each elixir is served in a two-ounce vial and guarantees at least an hour of mood enhancement. Find us on the web.

**Ivana:** You can find the link to Enhancing Elixirs' website in today's show notes. Use the promo code CREEK7 to get fifteen percent off your first order.

**Athena:** All right, we're back and ready to meet our guest.

**Ivana:** For anonymity our guest today will be known as Youngling. Can you test your mic out for us?

**Youngling:** Test. Test. One. Two.

**Ivana:** Sounds great.

**Athena:** Well, here we are. I know we're ready to jump into this interview. We have so many questions we want to ask. But there's just one thing. We thought you said you had something to show us.

**Youngling:** I did.

**Athena:** Well, where is it?

**Youngling:** I think I made a mistake. I don't have it anymore.

**Ivana:** Why not?

**Youngling:** I meant I think this is all a mistake. I was just joking about what I said. I thought it'd be funny.

**Athena:** You said it was a book, didn't you? Can you explain what the book looked like? What made it special?

**Youngling:** I'm going to take this off, all right?

**Athena:** You promised us an interview.

**Ivana:** You saw them, didn't you?

**Athena:** Who?

**Ivana:** The Bookish Witch and the New Girl. I caught a glimpse of them when we got on the elevator. They had a book.

**Athena:** The Bookish Witch. Of course.

**Ivana:** The bookshop...

**Athena:** We've never done our due diligence. We haven't shopped there. We didn't see the proof was there before our eyes the whole time.

**Youngling:** I don't know what you two are talking about, but I'd like for you to leave.

**Athena:** Oh, we've got everything we needed. You heard that right folks. Two real witches swooped in—probably on their brooms—to stop our interview. We have them on the ropes.

**Ivana:** But you know they won't talk to us now.

**Athena:** Who said anything about talking?

## 27

## THE RESTRICTED SECTION

"You're sure we shouldn't ask Lauren for help?" I asked.

Gran and Trish were adamant that we shouldn't.

"I know what you're thinking," Trish said. "But it's not about trusting her—which again, I'm not sure I do. It's just I think we should do this potion ourselves. It's straightforward enough."

"Straightforward?" Gran snorted. "I think you should have another look. It reveals more of itself every time I read it. It's not really a potion per se. And not a spell either. It's a bit of both."

The book was open on the kitchen table. We'd flipped through it in search of what it was that would enable me to talk to my father again. There was also one contender—a half potion, half spell that promised to temporarily rip my soul from my body.

But it wasn't *that* easy. And like Gran had said, things kept getting added with each glance at the page, almost as if we were the underaged witches.

Gran's gnarled finger hovered over the page. She pointed to the incantations at each step. Not all potions had such things. In fact, every one I'd seen so far—which was quite a few because of my research—had only entailed mixing ingredients over a hot cauldron and allowing them to bubble into sludge.

Trish leaned over to look at the page again. "You're right. It's a *spotion*."

This drew Gran's ire. "Never say that word again while I'm alive."

Trish shot me a smile. The word *spotion* was bound to be an inside joke between us for some time to come. I hid my smile and poked my head between theirs. Three heads above one book.

"This wasn't there before." My finger found the page. "There's a cost."

"I don't see it yet," Trish said.

"Me either." Gran stared and tried to will the words to show for her. "Ah, there it is. That's not good. No. No. I don't think this is a good idea."

"What does it say?" Trish asked.

"It says there are two paths. One is to find a demon, the same one as in the luck potion, Beruth, and have her stir. Demons have the power to pull a spirit through the shadow realm. So, if we use her, there's no cost."

"Aside from calling a demon," Gran spat.

"What's the cost?" Trish asked.

"That's the other path," I said. "If I stir the potion, then it costs me one year of my life because the end of a life is the other path to the shadow realm."

"Morbid," Trish said. "Is this really worth it?"

"I think so," I said. "It's not like we're any closer to

figuring out who killed him. And he still might be able to give me information about my mom."

"You know who killed him," Gran said. "Lauren did it whether she meant to or not."

"Her magic did. It doesn't mean she was responsible."

"There are other ways to find this information," Gran said.

I brushed her off and returned to the book. "It says to make it on sacred ground. Does that mean we have to haul a cauldron up to the graveyard?"

Gran looked like she wasn't going to answer. I gave her a look. I wasn't submitting. I wasn't reconsidering. I was going to make this *spotion* no matter the cost.

"I've done it a few times," Gran acknowledged.

"And another reason not to use Lauren's factory," Trish added. "There's nothing sacred about a vacant lot owned by a car dealership."

"Fair enough."

More words appeared on the page. I read them, then Gran found them. "It says here you'll need a guide—and it *can't* be a familiar."

"That must be the help Mr. Caulfield offered," I said. "It's like he knew."

"You're going to entrust your soul to a dead vampire?" Gran was more displeased by the minute.

"No. I don't have to trust him. But if Cyrus does, it's good enough for me." I changed the subject. "What about these ingredients? Do we have them?"

I scanned the list and shuddered, after all, this was something I was going to ingest. "Hairs of a hairy frog—"

"Not actual hairs by the way." Trish grimaced.

"Dried vomit of a sea cucumber. The tooth of a primate? This is disgusting!"

"It's one of the worst I've seen." Trish nodded. "Plus, I'm running low on some of these. And I don't have—"

"Don't you two worry your pretty little heads," Gran interjected. "I've got a whole monkey's jaw in the attic. And the rest, we can manage."

"You have a monkey's jaw? In the attic?"

Gran shrugged. "It's best to be prepared. Now, what does it say about the conditions?"

I read over the instructions again. So did Trish.

"It looks like we'll need to be at this step—" She dragged her finger down the page. "—by the witching hour. So, we should start it by sundown, I think."

Gran agreed. "And it only works from the witching hour to dawn. That's not a lot of time."

"It's more than enough," I said.

I read it over again. And more words appeared on the page.

"It says for best results, brew on a full moon. Rain is good. Lightning better. A cloudless sky can ruin it. What does that mean?"

Gran scowled. "It means we need the weatherman to be wrong about this weekend."

∼

Having to wait a whole week nagged at me. While we were inching closer to figuring things out, the killer was probably up to schemes of their own to thwart us. I had to be ready for another hex or a curse or whatever else.

Every time I thought we were about to solve the mystery, a new problem beyond my magical comprehension appeared. Magic isn't easy. Anyone who believes magic is the solution to life's problems is delusional.

For a long time, I'd been delusional.

Tuesday at the bookstore started off dull. I had little to do except read the spell again. And again. And again. But no new information popped up.

There was no question. We weren't using a demon this time. We had enough trouble with Brad, and we weren't going to add another potential issue to the mix.

There was just the slight problem of it costing me a year of my life to do so. Three hundred and sixty-five and one quarter days less than the hidden number known only to the keepers of such things—the grim reapers or fate or whoever.

It couldn't be all that bad. At least now I knew there was a life after death. *Something.* While still an unknown, it wasn't quite as big a question mark.

I kept Merritt's book on my side of the counter and flipped through the pages a few more times. The *spotion* was the only thing I found worthwhile. That was typical of these books. Half the pages were copies of copies. The same potions, the same spells and incantations passed from one witch to another. They listed common witching ingredients, herbs, and the like. Some discussed symbolism in nature, others told ghost stories, while others recorded witching lines as they passed from daughter to daughter. These were as dry a read as the book of Genesis—and a lot less murdery.

This book had one of those. Her grandmother had scrawled the name Merritt underneath Merritt's mother's name, a name she'd crossed out completely.

After about an hour, I was ready to fill some orders and find a better book from the used shelves. Maybe I could find something my dad would like and slip it under my spirit wings before my soul got ripped from my body.

*Probably best not to think about that.*

I got through three orders before the door chimed.

I leaned over the counter to get a view of the door.

"Oh, it's *you*." I stuffed Merritt's book under the shelf.

"It's me," pointy-faced Summer Shields said.

She went straight past the regular books and into the section of magic books. The real ones. She picked one at random and brought it to the counter.

"I'd like to purchase this, please."

I blinked. There wasn't an established protocol for something like this. Random people off the street never came in and asked for magic books. I knew this book wasn't meant for Summer, but could I stop her from buying it? It was like my first conversation with Merritt but reversed.

At least we'd know where it was if someone came looking for it. I decided to try and ring her up, knowing full well that the tablet register wasn't real—knowing that Trish had spelled it to look and perform the way it does.

I scanned the sticker placed inside every book, magic or otherwise. *Not authorized for sale*, it read on the tablet screen. So, Trish had a protocol. I just wasn't aware of it.

I told Summer as much.

"Fine," she snapped. And she got another book.

The same result—not authorized.

She tried one more time.

Then she raised her voice. "Are you telling me I'm not allowed to shop here? If so, I think that's newsworthy—enough for my real job."

"I'm not saying that," I said. "Try one of these."

She picked up a random mystery book from the shelf closest to the register. I scanned it. "Two dollars."

"I don't want this book," she sneered. "I want one of those."

"I'm sorry. I'll have to talk to Trish. Maybe something in our system is busted."

"You know full well that something in your system is *not* busted. You're doing this on purpose. We have the same rights to those books as any of you. Unless you want to admit it. Go ahead. Tell me you're a real witch, and I'll leave."

"I think you should leave," I said.

"You're playing with fire." Summer had said those words to me before.

"Listen. If you want this book, it's two dollars."

She glowered at me. Then she snatched the *other* book from beside the register—a magic book. Without an authorization for sale.

And she ran for the door.

She only made it a few steps outside before she screamed so loud I had to see what had happened.

The vape shop owner had come out to see what was going on too.

Summer was on the ground in the middle of the sidewalk, screaming and crying. And cursing—there was a lot of cursing. A lot of calling me names.

Summer's hair had fallen out, scattered on the ground. She was as bald as me. Trish's wards. They worked.

The wind picked up. Her hair fluttered down the street like feathers on the breeze.

## 28

## CAULDRON BUBBLE

The weather was glorious the whole rest of the week. Well, glorious by summer in Virginia standards. But by midday the next Saturday, it was raining buckets. And there was no letup in sight. The weatherman was wrong. Again. And Summer Shields hadn't shown up on TV all week. She hadn't made good on her threat to me either.

Lightning cracked outside, so close I could feel it. The thunder was like cannons. We cozied up, Gran and Stevie and me, watching TV most of the day. Anticipation for the night stretched every show, every commercial, every clap of thunder.

Trish stopped by about an hour before sundown. If you went by the overcast sky, it was hard to tell when that should be. Praise the internet.

She and Gran began to gather ingredients and put them next to the cauldron, beside the backdoor with a couple of umbrellas. While we weren't going to melt in water, we didn't want to get soaking wet either.

"I'm still unsure about this potion. And I *know* it's not a good idea." Gran took one last look at the book, resigned to help us no matter her opinion.

Thunder rumbled in the distance and there was a knock on the door.

Gran jerked her head from the book, and Trish asked me, "You invite someone else?"

I shook my head.

"You're sure it's not Lauren? I know she's *amazing* at potions."

"I'm sure," I said uncertainly.

I was totally unsure. I'd been friendly to Lauren. We'd even exchanged a few texts. She told me her business was off to a good start and asked if I wanted to help. I told her I had too much on my plate right now. I wasn't lying.

"Maybe it's that girl Merritt then." Trish made a face. "She added me as a friend on Facebook and liked about every post I've ever made."

"That's weird."

"What's so weird about liking things?" Gran asked.

"You don't let someone know you're stalking their timeline as soon as they friend you," Trish said.

"We don't have time for this conversation." I went to the door.

Lightning burst too close for comfort, spurring more urgent knocking. I opened it.

"Dave?"

Dave and his girls were huddled on the porch. He sheltered them, allowing them the awning and taking the brunt of the rain on his back. His black hair was beaded with raindrops and his face glistened.

"Hey, Constance," he said warily. "Are you busy tonight?"

THE GIRLS SHIVERED as the air conditioning in Gran's house hit them.

Dave barely crossed the threshold. "You remember when you said you wouldn't mind keeping them on a full moon—if I needed it?" he asked.

"I remember..."

"You did?" Trish, who'd followed me into the living room, arched an eyebrow toward her purple streak.

I rolled my eyes. "Don't worry about Trish. She's needed in the kitchen, I think."

"I'm not," Trish said, staying put.

"It's just, we kind of have plans tonight."

Dave sighed. "Yeah, well everyone seems to have plans tonight. Jared took the boys to a baseball tournament in Richmond. And Mrs. Mitchell forgot to tell me that her son is getting married this weekend."

"What about Willow?"

"Willow's working tonight." Dave made a face like his girls did before bedtime. "I really don't know where else to turn. No pun intended. It's just one night. Mrs. Mitchell gets back tomorrow."

I sighed and asked Trish, "What do you think?"

She thought about it. "You have to be up there. You're the one with the gifts—enhanced potion making and all that other stuff. Plus, you have to stir. I guess I can keep the kids."

"You're serious?" Dave asked.

"I wouldn't give her too much longer to think about it," I told him.

"Good enough for me." He smiled tentatively. "I'll see y'all first thing in the morning. And Trish... make sure you keep them in one piece."

Trish rolled her eyes. "Later, Sheriff. Howl at the moon for me."

Dave wasn't gone two minutes before the girls were begging to go with me and Gran to the graveyard.

"Why not?" Trish argued for them. "It'll be fun."

I blinked. "Your definition of fun and mine are different. They'd prefer a Disney movie, I'm sure."

"No, we wouldn't," Allie said.

"Really?" I scoffed. "We're going to get drenched in the rain waiting for hours for a potion to bubble in a graveyard in the middle of the woods. What part of that sounds fun to you three?"

"It does sound pretty boring," Allie admitted.

"It sounds creepy," Kacie said and tickled Elsie's middle.

Elsie smiled her missing tooth smile. "It does!"

"Fine." Allie sighed. "Okay. I want to go too."

I shook my head. "The answer's still no."

Trish fake coughed. "Uh hum. I am their babysitter. And I say they can go. But on one condition."

They looked at her blankly.

"They do everything I ask them to do. They don't whine. And they call me Trish, not Miss Lester."

"Okay, Trish." Elsie smiled again.

"I kinda like them," Trish whispered.

I rolled my eyes. "If anything happens to them…"

"Nothing's going to happen." Another bolt of lightning cracked outside. Trish made a face. "Okay… I'll spell them so they won't take on water or get hit by lightning."

"Do me while you're at it," I told her.

We set out down the path in the woods. Gran pointed and levitated the cauldron, leading it like a balloon tied to her finger. With the wards that Gran had put up, the graveyard now looked like more woods, indistinguishable from the rest. Still, we remembered to spell for hidden devices or spies.

But with the weather, chances were low that Summer and Jade would show. Gran put the wards up again behind us just in case.

And we got to work. We gathered fallen branches from the oak tree, spelled them dry, and Gran lit a water-resistant green flame at the cauldron's base.

The main ingredient in every potion is water. And that we had by the bucket. It only took a few minutes to direct enough rain into the giant pot.

We chanted the first spell as I sprinkled in the first few additions—those *must have* parts of frogs that make any potion do what they do. Next came the dried sea cucumber vomit. *Yum!* The simmering water turned a pinkish shade of orange.

"Neat!" the girls exclaimed.

But waiting another hour or so for the next phase of the *spotion* was as boring as we told them it would be. They climbed the tree. It looked like fun. Then they played a game of hide and seek, darting around the gravestones. Trish and I both partook this time, although Gran didn't seem to find it amusing. She'd brought a lawn chair and tried to watch an episode of *The Office* on her tablet underneath an umbrella.

Finally, it came time for the next ingredient and the next spell. The dark clouds parted, revealing the whole of the moon. The girls howled at it playfully.

Her hands in her pockets, Gran frowned.

"What? They're just playing."

"It's not that," she huffed. "The darn monkey's tooth. I must've dropped it."

"We can go back for it..."

"There isn't time," Trish said. "Why didn't you say something earlier?"

The old woman scowled.

"Can you just spell it here?" I asked her.

"I already tried summoning it."

"And it didn't work?" Trish asked.

Gran shook her head.

Trish scoured the tree line. "That would mean someone else has it…"

"Podcasters." Even if they couldn't find the graveyard, didn't mean they weren't out there looking. I couldn't believe the rain hadn't kept them away. I grimaced. "I'm not sure what the alternative is."

"You need a tooth?" Elsie asked.

We turned. "We do," I said. "But it doesn't look like you have any to spare."

She smiled again. There were so many missing teeth. "I wiggled it out this morning. But dad says the tooth fairy would only come to *our* house. He told me to keep it in my pocket until then."

"She's very particular that way." Trish nodded.

"If I let you use it, could I get it back?"

I shook my head. "I'm afraid not. How much does the Tooth Fairy normally leave under your pillow?"

"A dollar," Elsie said.

"What if we give you five dollars?" Trish asked her.

Elsie grinned and dug in her pocket. There, with a bit of lint, was a small tooth.

"Okay." Elsie did her best Jerry Maguire impression. "Show me the money."

## 29

## IN WITCH I TAKE FLIGHT

Once the tooth was swallowed by the bubbling gook, the girls lost interest. Trish accompanied them back to Gran's house with promises of a movie and ice cream.

*Don't count on any Rocky Road.*

Gran and I worked on the potion with spells and more ingredients. That was until the witching hour when I had to stir and stir and stir like it was a hollandaise. That hour burned off more than just a year of my life.

The potion bubbled, turning from orange to green to blue and finally to that brown color with the sludgy consistency of properly made potions, just like the luck potion and the one that healed my wounds from the hex.

And since most of the water had boiled away, the cauldron contained just enough for one use. Gran ladled it into a mason jar.

"Well, here you are." She eyed it skeptically. "I'm guessing you'll take your maiden voyage tomorrow night?"

"Actually," I said, "I told Mr. Caulfield to meet me tonight."

"You invited a ghost?" Gran looked displeased. "Little wolf girls, and now the ghost of a vampire. You've turned my home into a halfway house for the paranormally broken."

"Everything will be right as rain tomorrow," I told her. "It's only a day away."

"Wrong again," she said. "It's already today and I feel no better about it. Now, help me get these things together."

Ghosts rest during the witching hour. From midnight to one o'clock, their forms are at peace somewhere—neither in our world or the shadow realm.

I wanted to hurry to meet him. Helping Gran took up precious moments I could be spending with my dad.

We gathered what was left of the supplies, tucking them into the cauldron, and she floated it into the sky. I held the jar of potion to my chest protectively, and we set off.

"You know Stevie's just outside the gate," Gran said. "I assume he's accompanying you and your ghost friend? Or have you asked?"

"I'd hardly call Mr. Caulfield a friend," I said. "And you read what the instructions said, Stevie isn't allowed to accompany me."

"Not all the way," Gran agreed. "But he may be useful in the shadow realm, should you need him."

"When you say it like that, I guess I'd appreciate it if Stevie tagged along..."

"Then you should ask him yourself. He'd appreciate a request this time. You know if I ask him, he's bound to do it."

"I, uh, I didn't know that."

"Part of their contract," Gran said grimly. "Some witches treat their familiars like servants. It's shameful, really."

I nodded. That did sound shameful. I reflected on my own short relationship with Brad. Had I ever *demanded* something of him? Was a request from me the reason he wound up a prisoner to that demon?

Again, I found myself comparing the real witching world to the one I knew from books. The job of a familiar was complex. But necessary?

And now Gran had put the comparison with a house-elf in my mind. I wondered, could familiars be freed of their bonds?

We made our way back to Gran's house, and along the way, I asked Stevie if he'd accompany me.

He agreed in his *familiar* snarky way.

The monkey's jaw was on the kitchen table. Trish pretended to be wide awake. She stretched her eyes wide a few times and went to make some tea. Gran lowered the cauldron into the corner beside the garage door.

I tiptoed past the kitchen and through the living room. It was so late. And so dark. Except for the blue luminescence at the doorway. The ghost of Mr. Caulfield was at the threshold.

"I can't come inside unless the caster of these wards allows me to," he said when I opened the door for him.

"Gran," I called.

"Fine. Fine. You may enter, for one day and one day only."

"You're so kind." His blurry ghost face rolled its eyes. "I hadn't planned to make haunting this place a habit."

"It's for my own protection," Gran said archly. "You haven't seen me in my nightgown yet."

Trish busted a gut.

Back in the kitchen, I noticed she'd failed to make me a cup. "You shouldn't have anything with the *spotion*. And just so you know, the girls are bunking in your room upstairs. I hope you don't mind—it seemed like the best place."

"Right." That meant I had to find another place to park my body while I was gone.

I eyed the mason jar in my hand with some trepidation.

*Yuck!*

"Take it and lie down on the couch," Trish said. "We can watch over your body for the night."

"You can," Gran told her. "I need my beauty sleep."

"Fine. *I'll* watch over your body. But left to my own devices, you might wake up with Sharpie all over your face."

I feigned a chuckle, focusing on her joke instead of the fact that my soul was about to be ripped from my body.

"Just remember," I said, "there are children with eyes upstairs. No phallic symbols. And they wake up at the crack of dawn."

Trish winced. "Of course they do. Cuteness comes at a price."

A price—another reminder of that year I'd just given up. *Poof. Gone.*

"Take good care of them," I said. "I should be back before they wake up."

Like forcing a stubborn child to take gross medicine, my stomach threatened to expel its contents before the jar even touched my lips. I got shaky and nervous, like I do after giving blood. Only there was no orange juice and cookie.

There was only this nasty brown sludge. I glowered at it.

Part of the problem was the taste. And the feel. And the burn. I knew what they felt like now—too well. And it wasn't a pleasant feeling.

The other, weightier, issue was the effects of the potion. *Will it hurt?* Souls and bodies kind of belong together, don't they?

*Best not to dwell on it.*

Except I did dwell on it. So much that I almost dropped the jar when my arm spasmed. A subconscious warning?

Trish saw it coming. She grabbed my arm at the shoulder and the elbow and steadied me.

"It's going to be okay." She maneuvered the jar to my lips and held it there. "This is what you want, right? You don't *have* to do this."

"I want to tell him goodbye," I sobbed.

"I know what you want. But is it really what you need?"

I struggled.

*It is... isn't it?*

There are certain people worth going back for.

Anyone with this kind of power would use it. *Wouldn't they?*

I eased the jar forward and allowed gravity to do its job.

The air whooshed out of my lungs. The last time it happened—when I'd had the wind knocked out of me—the air had come back.

Not this time.

I felt the burning. From head to toe. It burned so badly.

I fell, and Trish guided my body down to the couch only for me to realize I was still standing. Right where I had been. I was as blue and indistinct as Mr. Caulfield.

He regarded me with interest. "It takes some getting used to."

Gran frowned. "You only have until sunrise."

I should've planned this better. I could've waited until tomorrow. I could have had more time.

"Follow me." Mr. Caulfield ghosted through the backdoor and I followed. Stevie darted after us, sending the cat door flapping.

The clouds were blocking out the full moon again. I

caught myself listening for a howl in the distance, even knowing that Dave was probably miles outside the city.

An owl hooted a warning as we brushed the tops of trees.

Below us, Stevie's form shifted to shadow, growing larger. It writhed and twisted as he sped along a makeshift path beneath us.

"I know of only two working portals to the shadow realm within the city proper," Mr. Caulfield called over the rushing air. "There's only one at the vineyard."

"Where to then?" I shouted.

"You know the park by the library? It's the closest."

That made sense. The park was where I met Brad for the first time. I didn't have a stomach, but guilt seeped into something resembling it.

I had to put more effort into getting him back.

I pushed the thought away, making myself feel even more guilty.

"Where are the other portals?" I asked.

"In the back of Trish's bookstore. There used to be one at the old courthouse, but it's closed off somehow. No way in or out."

We flew down toward the park's gates. The swing set where I'd first met Dave's girls gleamed in the orange light of a streetlamp.

"Do you see it?" Mr. Caulfield asked.

At first, the answer was no. Not until Stevie's shadow flickered across the highway making a beeline to... it looked like a black hole in front of a giant oak not unlike the one in the graveyard.

The edges of the void were traced with wisps of purple and blue energy turning clockwise and pulsing every few seconds.

Stevie vanished into it. Mr. Caulfield's flight path took him straight toward it without slowing.

I hovered outside the portal, uncertainty holding me back. It felt like a leap of faith—like a quantum leap. The leap home. The leap to see my father again.

## 30

## IN WITCH I VISIT THE SHADOW REALM

As I passed through the portal into the shadow realm, a weight caught me and forced my legs to the ground. It made my would-be knees buckle. Only moments before, I'd been a ghost, flying and free. *A spirit.* Now I was matter again, not just energy.

I blinked.

I was in the same park. Or *almost*. The world was black and white like an old TV show. Like my annual viewing of *Casablanca*.

The shadows were more sinister. They had a jaggedness and didn't match the shape of their object—the tree, the gate. There was no swing set in the shadow realm. No light source either. So how there were shadows was beyond me.

So mesmerized by the subtle differences, I'd failed to notice the bigger changes. Not until one stepped into view. Mr. Caulfield looked like Mr. Caulfield—more like the one I'd known on Earth, a few years removed. Being a vampire, that meant several hundred.

He wore a suit.

I looked down to see that I was also clothed in the attire

I'd been wearing at home. But it was more like the memory of those clothes, not the real things. The jeans were right, but the logo and design on my t-shirt was all sorts of wrong. It changed before my eyes, coming much closer to the real thing until my mind struggled to remember the finer details.

Even my hair was like a memory of my wig. That is until I thought about it and my natural thick strands, a tad frizzy, not blonde but the black and white equivalent, morphed into existence.

Those changes paled in comparison to the biggest thing I'd missed.

A statue—or what I'd mistook for a statue—moved. Stevie. A beautiful man stood before my eyes, wearing—I did a double take—a toga. A rather short toga that draped over one shoulder and left the other one bare. His shoulders, his chest, his arms, even his neck could have been chiseled from stone. His facial features too—sharp cheekbones, a cleft in his chin.

A pair of wings extending from his back were the only imperfections I could see. Torn, feathers tattered or missing, enough to expose scarred skin and some of the underlying skeletal structure.

Still, I was awed by his beauty. Of what he was. A fallen angel.

"Stop staring, Constance. It's rude."

"I don't know. I agree with *her* eyes," Mr. Caulfield said. "It's a bit unnerving seeing you like that."

"I can't be a cat all the time, now can I?" Stevie's sneer broke the spell. He might look different, but he was the same sardonic familiar.

"So, how does this work?" I asked.

I couldn't shake the weirdness of going from ghost form to this false body. I pinched the skin on my arm, and it hurt.

Stevie said, "Any door or gate in this realm will open to any world you wish it to—or any world you know exists. But only these portals into the shadow realm itself lead to the realm we know as Earth."

"Okay," I said. "That sounds simple enough."

He nodded. "The beauty is in its simplicity. It's perfect in that way. This is how it's supposed to work: a reaper escorts the soul to the shadow realm and shows the spirit a door.

"They tell the spirit that the afterlife lies on the other side of that door. The soul usually has a picture of what they believe the afterlife to be. Sometimes that's a shared picture—you'll find many Christians together in realms they call heaven. And if they weren't so good on Earth, and believed themselves not to have met certain criteria..."

"Then they go to hell?" I asked.

"To a bad place, of sorts. The good thing is the majority of people who believe this truly deserve it. And don't fret, your dad isn't one of them."

"Will the gate work?" I pointed at the park's gate.

"It will," Mr. Caulfield said. "But you can't just wish to see your father and find him there. It's not that easy. That's why I'm here."

"I don't get it."

"You can't just wish it and then be wherever your father is."

"That's just a recipe for creating a world of your own," Stevie said. "A world made up of memories of your father."

"With you here," Mr. Caulfield said, "I should be able to point us in the right direction. Your souls are linked. This is why you need me here—to be your guide through the afterlife."

"Thank you for doing this," I said.

Mr. Caulfield headed for the gate. "Now, each of you put a hand on one of my shoulders and follow me."

∽

WE PASSED through the gate into in a world of vivid color—mostly green. Rolling hills stretched to a great forest of exotic trees and lush green foliage.

The other colors were present too when I examined the world more closely—wildflowers along the cobblestone path that we were standing on, blue sky, rays of the yellow light from a hidden sun. On the horizon, almost too distant to see, a dark gray mountain touched the clouds.

It was a Tolkien dream. Like the shire, only brighter. I felt the urge to shield my eyes from it but realized there was no need. It wasn't my eyes being dazzled—it was my spirit reacting to the sheer beauty of the world.

Neither Mr. Caulfield nor Stevie commented on it. They continued walking, and I followed until out of nowhere, a man barred us from going further.

White bearded and wearing a tunic of the same color, he held a wooden staff horizontally across the cobbles. Going around him meant treading on the lush greenscape and somehow, that wasn't an option.

The land had magical protection of its own.

"Who enters this realm?" the man asked us.

"Visitors," Mr. Caulfield said. "Just visiting."

"One of the fallen?"

"I'll wait here," Stevie said.

"And her?" The man poked the staff into my chest. "Is *she* just visiting?"

"Today she is," Stevie told him.

The man backed away, vanishing in a way that made me wonder if he'd even been there in the first place.

"That was weird."

"Gatekeeper," Stevie said. "All the *good* realms have one."

"Some of the bad ones too," Mr. Caulfield drawled. "They're part of the changes made after Cyrus's departure. Come on. You father's cottage is this way."

Given the wide open spaces, I expected to be walking for some time. But our steps and the world around us weren't aligned in that manner. A small house appeared on a nearby hill connected by a path of its own—this one, a single row of stones that we followed up the hill.

Mr. Caulfield stepped aside and gestured toward the door. "I'll wait for you here."

"I'll be quick." I knew it was a lie as soon as I uttered the words.

"Time here is not time at all," Mr. Caulfield said. "We can't check a watch and know when to return."

"I said I'll be quick."

"But you didn't mean it. And it's not about being quick. Places like this—for mortals like us—try to draw you in. It will try to keep you here like you're another soul for its collection. When you start to feel that happening, then you'll know it's time to leave."

"Okay." I had no clue what he meant, but I rolled with it.

I knocked on the door. It was answered in seconds, not shyly either. My father opened it wide. When his eyes met mine, his reserved smile became a grin.

"Constance? What are you... Why... Is it really...?"

"It's me, Dad."

"You shouldn't be here." His grin said otherwise. "But I'm glad you are. Come in. Come in. And you as well. Everyone's welcome."

"Are you sure?" Mr. Caulfield asked me, not my father.

I nodded. "He says it's okay."

Despite the modest exterior, the cottage was filled with modern amenities. Except for a TV. He'd never cared much for television. I assumed that if he wanted one, one would be there.

The living room had bookshelves on every wall, all overflowing. This furniture looked like the most comfortable furniture imaginable—a seat for every reading position.

"Sit down," he said. "I'll make you some tea."

The kettle whistled as soon as he put it on the burner. I began to understand what Mr. Caulfield meant about time.

He handed out cups, then turned his attention to me.

"You're here," he said. "I'd be lying if I said I wasn't happy to see your face. To hear your voice. So often I find myself living in my memories. This is better."

"I'm glad to see you too, Dad."

"What do you think of my idea of heaven?"

"It looks like heaven," I said.

Dad's face was worried. "Sweetheart, what did this visit cost you?"

"Why does it matter?" I asked. "I wanted to see you. So, I'm here."

"It matters because your life is all that matters," Dad said. "You don't owe me anything. Not a goodbye. And you definitely don't need to worry yourself over my death. It is what it is. Now, tell me what this little trip cost you."

"A year," I said. "It cost me a year. That's all."

"That's all?" He shook his head. "Constance, that's—"

"It's nothing," I shot back. "Why does my life matter when it ends like this?" I gestured to the room.

His face fell. I felt worse than those few times in my teenage years when I'd disappointed him.

We never had arguments. No, it was worse than that. We had discussions that ended when I needed to cry. When I felt so bad for what I'd done, he didn't have to worry about me doing it again.

"I'll just be here with you," I said. "What's one year?"

"That's not how this works." His eyes begged Mr. Caulfield for support.

"What your father means is that the afterlife is solitary. Your soul is resting. It had its time—time to be with family, to be with friends. And here, you're supposed to be at peace."

"But that's not fair!" I glared at Mr. Caulfield. "You had a thousand years on earth, and now you get to parade around as a spirit."

"And I'm sure it will *cost* him in the end," Dad said. "And he's aware of that."

Mr. Caulfield nodded. "Ghosts don't stick around forever."

"Well, I'm here now," I told my dad. "That year is gone. There's nothing I can do about it. I came here to see you, so let me."

"But why?" he asked.

"To see... to see if you knew who killed you."

"You know that I do not."

"Then," I struggled for words, "I came to say goodbye."

"Those aren't the only reasons."

Yes there was another reason, but I wanted this to be about him. And now it wasn't. He was always so good at these *Growing Pains* style talks, like he'd read a book by Dr. Jason Seaver.

"You don't have enough time for me to coax it out of you, sweetheart. Get whatever it is off your chest."

"It's about Mom," I said.

Now, knowing what the afterlife entailed—that this was the last time I would see him—I didn't want to ask these questions anymore. I just wanted to be with him.

My mom wasn't here. She was somewhere in the world. It made here and now more pressing.

"Go on," he urged.

"I wanted to know"—my voice threatened to crack—"if you remember anything about when Mom disappeared. About the Faction—that organization she was working for."

He began to shake his head.

"Okay, you don't. It's not a big deal. I was just surprised when you said you knew she was a witch."

"You should try to remember," Mr. Caulfield urged. "Your memories are more vivid now."

Still shaking his head, Dad was on the verge of saying "no" when his eyes went wide.

"There *was* someone," he said. "I remember. She said she was from the studio. She didn't know that I knew anything. And I played along because I thought it was your mom's cover. But now I realize, it was hers. *She* was pretending."

"Who?" I asked.

"She told me she was investigating your mother's disappearance. That perhaps they could find the plane's wreckage. I blew her off. And I never saw her again."

"Do you remember her name?"

"Maybe?" He struggled. "It was a funny name. Different."

He closed his eyes, reliving the memory. "Yeah. Different. I thought maybe her parents had been hippies. It was something... something like Rainbow."

## 31

## IN WITCH I NEVER WANT TO LEAVE

Suddenly, a weight lifted off my shoulders.

I'd figured it out—or he had. Dad had solved his own murder.

It was Kalene. It had to be.

Her mom had worked for the Faction. That was it. It was so simple. How had I not seen it before?

*Government jobs*, I thought. *Or a front for an organization bent on controlling the world's population of witches. An organization that didn't want me to know what really happened to my mother.*

I could leave happy. I had the information I'd come for —but the thought of leaving wasn't a happy one.

"I take it you know that name?"

I nodded.

Rainbow—as in Kalene's mom. As in Kalene's deceased mom. She'd been burned in the Creel Creek Courthouse fire.

And she used Lauren, giving the unwitting witch her mother's potion book. The spell book with its name inscribed in the pages. Beruth. Had Lauren called the demon...or did she have to?

Could Kalene set the demon on her the way it had been set on me in the car? With some hair and a look in the mirror? Or maybe she only had to touch the book—to read the name.

That was it. I'd never been hexed. I remembered how my eyes went red. And Lauren had worn those sunglasses. Had that been the demon?

But how did it deceive my witch instincts so easily?

"I've been so stupid," I said aloud.

"How so?" Mr. Caulfield asked.

"Lauren," I said.

"I thought you trusted her," Mr. Caulfield said.

"I do. Or I did. But she was possessed by a demon. And *it* took luck potion."

At her potion factory, I'd taken everything she said at face value. It was like she knew exactly what to say. The lies had rolled off her tongue so easily—just like they had for me and Trish when we got the book from Merritt.

"She lied and heck, she even sold me a car."

"Then who's to blame?"

"The demon?" I shrugged. "Or Kalene—who I assume is controlling it. Rainbow was her mother after all."

I explained about the fire and the connection to the Faction that Rainbow's appearance at both Gran's and dad's house must mean.

And when I was done, I was done. Done caring about life or death. What did his murder matter when he was right there in front of me?

"Well, it was a pleasure meeting you, Henry." Mr. Caulfield stood to leave, looking at me pointedly.

"I don't mean to run you off," Dad said.

"It's not me who needs running off." Mr. Caulfield tilted his head in my direction.

"Right. Right." Dad got up and came to give me a hug. "Sweetheart, it was lovely seeing you again. But it's time you…"

"Go?" I said sadly. "But we just got here. I haven't had any tea."

"And it's best you don't," Mr. Caulfield said.

Dad said, "He's a lovely man. I wish I'd known him on Earth."

"You *really* don't, Dad." To the former vampire, I asked, "Can I just have a few more minutes?"

He frowned. "You remember what we talked about?"

"I remember."

"And how are you feeling now?"

"Like I want to stay."

"And you remember what that means?"

"That I shouldn't."

They both nodded. Both had pity on their faces.

Then I remembered there were three girls waiting for me to wake up at Gran's house.

"I didn't even get to ask how *you* are," I told my dad.

"I'm a lot better now that I got to see you."

He wrapped me in the tightest of hugs. And I left with tears streaming down my cheeks.

It was hard saying goodbye.

Stevie was waiting on the path. The guard stayed a few paces ahead of him, waving his staff like a baton.

He nodded to us on our way out.

Then it was off through the shadow realm again, and I hastily explained my theory to Stevie. We made for the portal to the real world.

Mr. Caulfield went first.

But Stevie turned to me before stepping through. "You know, you're really going to need to light a fire under yourself to get back in time."

I stopped short.

*Fire!*

How many times had I thought about that word recently? Too many.

But had I ever really stopped and thought about it?

*How did such a powerful witch get killed in a fire? What really happened in that courthouse?*

"Stevie," I called. "Mr. Caulfield said that the courthouse used to have its own portal. But now it's closed. When did that happen?"

"Around ten years ago, I think. Why?"

*Why does that matter?*

I questioned my own thinking. *Is Kalene really to blame? Or had she been controlled by the demon too?*

*Those eyes.*

Lauren wore the sunglasses Kalene left behind. The sunglasses the demon didn't need anymore—not until it stole Lauren's body.

"I... I think I know where our demon is."

"You do, huh? I haven't fought a demon in ages."

"So, you'll help me?"

Stevie smiled mischievously. "I thought you'd never ask."

## 32

## DEMONIZED

Shooting in black and white had given shows like *The Addams Family* and *The Munsters* a gothic edge they'd never have gotten with color. The same could be said of the shadow realm. Everything was a shadowy mirror of the regular world. None of it looked quite right.

Stevie and I had gone from portal to portal—to Bewitched Books.

"Be right back," he said and stepped through to the real world.

Moments later, he returned with Twinkie. A gorgeous woman, taller than me—and that's saying something—with wings were less broken by the fall.

Again, I was mesmerized by beauty.

"This should be interesting." She all but cracked her knuckles.

I was going into this fight with the dream team, if only Brad were here. There was nothing Mr. Caulfield could contribute. He had no powers here, not like them. And not like me. He went to tell Gran and Trish what we learned.

But I was still putting the pieces together.

"There's one thing I don't understand," I said to them. "If there's been a demon right here this whole time, how come *you* didn't know it?"

"We're not all-powerful, Constance," Twinkie said. It was much harder to think of her as Twinkie in this form.

"In the mortal realm the magic is at *your* disposal, not ours. And here, while we do have magic, the fallen are on equal footing with angels, demons, and even the Fae."

"Granted," Stevie said, "we should've done more to find out the whys of that portal being concealed."

"If a demon wants to stay hidden," Twinkie said, "there's little we could do to stop it."

"The question is *why* do they want to be seen now?" Stevie mused.

"Well, I think it's time we find out."

Through the window of the shadow bookstore and down the street, the charred shell of the old courthouse was a silhouette against the graying sky. In the real world, it was almost dawn.

"What now?" Stevie asked. We were in front of the courthouse between two of the four remaining pillars, none of which was whole. This was originally the main entrance. Now, the building was open on all four sides, and the interior was a charred memory. How the dome over the rotunda was still there was a mystery. It reminded me of Lauren's potion factory.

*Is it really this simple?* I asked myself, reminded of the spell she'd taught us to undo the wards.

But here in the shadow realm, the magic was so raw the words weren't needed. With just a thought, the illusion glimmered away and the courthouse stood there as proudly as it once had.

A guttural scream came from inside the building.

"There goes the element of surprise," Stevie said.

I was careful going through the doors. I didn't think about anything, not wanting to inadvertently go to another realm. A stray thought about my dad could've easily sent us back to him.

I worked to push those thoughts away, focused instead on vengeance. Pretty soon I would be face to face with his killer. Of that, I was certain.

Only, it wasn't a demon we found in the lobby. It was an older woman. She looked a lot like Kalene did now, only her nose wasn't right. And her neck was too thin. The woman was laying in the middle of the floor with salt in a circle around her.

The shadow of the salt box was on the floor beside her. The room had been ransacked. Holes torn in the shadowy walls. Tables splintered. Shadows of books lying open, strewn across the room.

"Where is she?" Stevie hissed.

"Oh, she lurks about the building," the woman said. "She's so much stronger now than she was. Or I'm so much weaker." She smiled weakly.

Stevie and Twinkie took off in different directions, neither going straight through the rotunda.

"Who are you?" I asked. But I knew the answer.

"My name is Rainbow," she said, her voice even weaker than her smile. "It's nice to finally meet you, Constance Campbell."

"What is this place?"

"This has been my prison for the past ten years," she said. "Although, I'd been imprisoned in my own mind well before that."

The demon wailed again from somewhere in the

recesses of the building, perhaps in pain, perhaps with joy. It was hard to tell.

"Why did you let it out?" I asked.

Rainbow shook her head. "It's not what you think, dear. Allow me to explain."

What else could I do? I kneeled beside her and listened.

"Your mother took a job a long time ago. A job working for me."

"For the Faction," I corrected.

"Yes. The Faction. But they're not the sinister organization everyone believes them to be."

"Then what are they?"

"The righters of wrongs. The keepers of secrets." She gazed at the ceiling. "The seekers of truth."

"Then tell some truth," I challenged. "What happened to my mom?"

She had known this was coming, and she nodded. "We were working together to find and capture an escaped demon. You see, once a demon is loosed on the outside world, they're almost unstoppable. Once they're no longer bound to a circle, to a witch—no longer bound to the shadow realms—it's especially difficult to bind them back.

"Your mother and I, we were separated from our familiars." She could see a question on my lips and hushed me with a finger. "Then we got separated from each other. This was in London, a long time ago. I came back with a demon lodged in my mind. And your mother *never* returned at all."

"But you visited my dad—you visited Gran."

"She did." Rainbow's eyes darted toward the back of the courthouse. "Beruth wanted to make sure their plan had gone accordingly."

"Whose plan?"

"She never told me. Whoever allowed her to escape set this in motion. They wanted to infiltrate the Faction and bring it down from the inside. And their plan was working."

"Then what happened?" I asked. "How did you wind up here?"

"Demons enjoy their freedom. Being locked inside my mind wasn't freedom. Not what she was promised. She started to get bored with me. Bored with raising a grown-up daughter and a farm. Poor Kalene knew something was wrong, but it was before she came of age.

"One day, I woke up to find the demon had left me. Most of my memories were intact, even those with the demon. She wasn't gone long, just long enough for me to put together a plan. I decided to sacrifice myself should she leave me to my own devices again."

"And you were..."

"Beruth left me for a moment while at work. This place used to be where I kept many of the Faction's most prized books."

"You really were a bookkeeper."

"I really was a bookkeeper." She smiled again, and it could've been my imagination, but I thought it looked stronger.

"I carried out the plan. I conjured a fire to purify the building and went out in a blaze of glory, binding her spirit with mine.

"And for a while, I was able to keep her at bay, keep her locked here—bound with the last vestiges of my magic. Until slowly, it began to siphon my daughter's away."

"Kalene." I sighed.

"Every time she uses her magic, it gives the demon a window of opportunity—an escape through the magic. And here lately, she's had a lot of opportunity."

The coven with Lauren. Kalene had been using, or trying to use, magic more frequently.

"But why would Beruth kill my dad?"

"Probably because not so long ago, there was a visitor in town. We could only see its shadow as it walked through this place searching for something—of what I don't know. But its shadow looked a lot like Serena Campbell."

"My mom?" I gasped. "Do you think what happened to you happened to her?"

"I don't know," Rainbow said. "But I know her appearance set things in motion… again."

There were sounds of a scuffle. Then a roar and a hiss. They grew louder, filling the rotunda behind Rainbow.

"What does the Faction actually do?" I asked her.

"Think about what you've learned in your fortieth year so far. There's a reason we don't come of age until forty. A reason that familiars, angels, and demons exist. And a reason that vampires and werewolves can't control themselves—their powers—while others can. The Faction seeks that knowledge. But there are some who want to thwart them. Who want to keep the supernatural world a secret even from those who live inside it."

"Knowledge is power," I said.

"I wish I could give you more," Rainbow said. "You mother is out there somewhere, Constance. You must find her."

There was a cry of pain in the other room. Not from the demon. I recognized Stevie's bellow.

"What do we do about her?"

"The time has come when I must pass this burden to someone else," Rainbow said. "Once freed from my binding, she can use any door to leave this realm. You must not allow that to happen."

"What should I do?"

"You're a good witch," she said. "You'll think of something."

She had a lot of confidence in me. Almost as much as I had in myself.

I nodded. "I will."

I left her there and followed the noise. There was a melee going on. The two semi-angelic familiars fought against a demon transfigured to look more animal than angel, with horns, and hooves, and a long forking tail.

Her tail slashed through the air as she fought to counter blows from Stevie and magic from Twinkie. Then she shot fire from her mouth and struck Stevie in the chest. It did little harm to his body but his wings were singed from prior flames.

It gave Twinkie an opening. She tried to grapple, I think, locking up with the demon, but the beast threw her over its shoulders with ease.

Maybe they weren't such a dream team after all.

Stevie got up and dusted himself off, then jumped in. He was able to wrestle the demon to the ground.

I looked back at Rainbow, catching her eye and I nodded. It was time.

She eased herself from her circle of protection and a portal appeared. A portal that had been closed off for these ten years.

And free now, the spirit of Rainbow Moone could go anywhere she liked. She looked longingly at that portal.

"I can't go back to visit Kalene," she said. "I can't tell her how proud of her I am."

"But I can," I told her. "I can say those things. And I will."

Rainbow smiled. "You're a good witch, Constance Campbell. Make sure when you find your mother, you tell her I say so."

## 33

## THE WORST HEADACHE

Things weren't going well against the demon, Beruth. I tried to use my magic to help. But like the demon's fire on Stevie's chest, the magic had almost no effect. I could only watch and hope that the demon didn't get free. The familiars had done a decent job of closing off the exits in the back of the circular room. Her only way out was through me.

They tangled and twisted on the ground. Twinkie beat her broken wings madly, struggling against the demon.

Gray light flooded through the windows of the room onto the scrum. It was the shadow sun. I'd missed my chance to return to my body. Perhaps that meant I was stuck here forever, in this limbo like Rainbow had been.

I only took my eyes off the demon for a second, but it was long enough for it to realize it had a chance to escape. Somehow, she knew that Rainbow had left. And I was standing in the doorway to her freedom.

She gave voice to an evil roar, which caught me off guard. The familiars' hold on the demon failed, and she barreled at me like a bull charging a matador. And just like that, with the doorway my red cape, my instincts caused me to slip to the side.

She was partially through the door before I reacted again. I had no sword to stick in her back. I had no magic strong enough to stop her.

I reached out a hand and grabbed...something. I couldn't allow her to leave.

She fell horns first to the ground at my feet. I'd been able to catch her forked tail.

*Catch a demon by its tail*, I recalled Gran's little rhyme.

"Way to make it look easy," Stevie said.

"We'll take it from here." Twinkie took hold of the demon's tail and looked at the sky. "You really should be getting back."

I nodded, then ran back and slipped through the portal to my world.

My flight through town was uneventful except that the sun was much higher than I hoped it would be. I wondered what the extra minutes would mean.

Everyone was in the living room of Gran's house. And I mean everyone. Trish and Gran. Dave's girls and Dave, human again. Even Kalene was there.

They waited, anxious for my return. And I *tried* to return.

"She's here," Gran told those who couldn't see me.

"Constance?" Dave called.

He searched the room for my ghostly form but wasn't able to find me. The witches *could* see me. They could see my struggle.

But no matter how hard I tried, my body refused my spirit. The two just wouldn't connect.

Finally, Gran stood by my feet and pointed at my chest.

The ruby ring she always wore glinted in the sunlight. And she conjured a spell.

> "Mother Gaia hear my plea,
> Join the soul with the woman it used to be.
> This kind of magic can't be given for free,
> In payment take a year from me.
> A year from me you can take.
> A year from me, for goodness' sake.
> Give her life and give it now.
> Take that year, it is my vow."

THEY WAITED WITH BATED BREATH.

I waited.

*Did the spell work?*

I gasped, sucking in so much air I thought I was going to pass out as my soul joined my body.

My senses kicked in. I regained control of my limbs, then of my neck and chest. I tried to sit up.

And that's when this world introduced me to the pain, and I passed out.

~

SOME HOURS LATER—I didn't know how many—I was able to open my eyes but unable to do much else. It like that pain you get two days after a hard workout, worse than the day after—pain that makes your legs weak. The pain that keeps you from lifting your hands to wash your hair. In every inch of my body.

I couldn't move my neck because my head was a hundred-pound medicine ball. It wasn't just my muscles. My head throbbed from a migraine, piercing me between the eyes. My lips were dry. My mouth too.

Perhaps more worrisome than those being dry was my magic. The well, as I'd come to think of it, was bone dry. Not a trace of magic left—much worse after our binding of the demon in the garage. The day I'd last heard Brad's voice.

I rolled my eyes to see Gran in her recliner watching TV—or more accurately, to see Gran's fuzzy pink slippers pointing at the sky.

"You're finally awake, huh?"

"If you can call it that," I croaked.

"That boyfriend of yours has been back three times today," she said. "Trish has called twice. Kalene once. And even that pharaoh guy called asking about you. He wanted to know if he could bring us dinner made by his chef."

"I hope you said yes."

"Why would I—I'm perfectly capable of cooking a good meal."

Her idea of whipping up a meal consisted of adding an egg to a box of ingredients.

"I need water," I said.

"There's a bowl of ice chips beside you that have turned to water." I could hear the smile in her voice. "Almost like magic."

"Ice chips? Like when I was in the hospital?"

"You probably *should* be in a hospital," Gran said. "You were dead for about fifteen minutes. And your soul was out of your body much longer. How are you feeling?"

"Like I got run over by a truck."

"That *does* happen."

"Getting run over by a truck?" I found the bowl and sipped.

"Well, that too. I meant that there are bound to be consequences from a potion like that—especially when you *defied* its limits."

That's right. I had. But I wasn't the only one who paid for this.

I found enough strength to sit up. And I glared at her. The old woman stared back at me. Blue eyes. Gray hair. Fuzzy pink slippers.

"That spell," I said. "The one you used to bring me back. It cost *you* something. Didn't it?"

"A year—the same bargain you made to get there. I figured it'd be enough to bring you back."

"But Gran," I cried, "we have only have so much time."

If I'd learned anything in the little time with my father, it was that.

"I get what you're saying—" She frowned. "—that *I* only have so much time left. Trish thought so too. She thought maybe I'd up and die right there. Proved her wrong."

"Yeah, but—"

"It could be any time," Gran said sarcastically. "Now. Or now. Or now. Or maybe now."

She feigned falling back in her chair, closing her eyes and letting her tongue hang out to the side.

"When it *does* happen," I said, "I hope you don't look like that."

"I like how you use the word when—like you're stuck here forever."

"Are you saying I should move out?"

"I'm saying"—she waggled her finger at me—"that you're welcome to come and go as you please. I don't need a babysitter, a nanny, or a maid."

"At your age," I said, "they call them caretakers. And they're kind of a three-in-one deal. Now, tell me. Did you really turn down a meal from Cyrus's chef?"

Gran snorted. "It's on the table."

"It's *already* on the table? What time is it?"

"Late. You've been asleep all day."

I got up shakily and tottered to the kitchen table.

"Are you coming?" I asked Gran.

"I can't."

"Why not?"

"I lied to you earlier," she said weakly. "The magic I did to bring you back drained me. And I *also* feel like I was hit by a Mack truck."

## 34

## IN WITCH I SEE A FAMILIAR FACE

The next few days were tiring. And my magic was weak, if nonexistent. But Kalene's had come back with a vengeance. She popped by a few times and we talked. We talked about a lot of things—our mothers, the Faction, and the road to recovery.

I could see in her eyes that my message had opened fresh wounds where others had healed. We were both on paths to recovery. And both in a new search for answers.

*Who is the Faction? Who are its members? And why haven't they revealed themselves to us?*

After the fire, my mother's disappearance, and me turning forty, they'd had ample opportunities.

*Shouldn't someone have come forward by now?*

Kalene visits were occasional, Dave's were frequent. He finally asked the question. And I was finally able to answer.

"Constance," he said one afternoon, "this might sound a little awkward. I don't even know what they call it these days. Like I know we've been on dates but—"

"Yes," I said.

"I haven't even asked you."

"Fine, then ask me."

"Now it's gonna sound even more stupid."

"Even better." I smiled.

"Will you, uh, be my girlfriend?"

"Definitely," I said with a peck on his lips. "I'm only glad you didn't ask to go steady. *That* would've been awkward."

"Well, it crossed my mind."

"I bet it did." I smiled, and we kissed again.

Eventually, things got back to normal. There was just the original problem. Still no Brad.

On my first day back at the bookstore, I passed the shell of the courthouse and took the next turn a little too fast and a bottle rolled out from under the seat.

Thankfully, it didn't cause another accident.

I reached down and fished the bottle of luck potion Lauren had brewed from the floor.

That sparked a memory of a demon using it to say the right words.

"Huh," I said aloud. "I wonder if that would work in reverse."

Gran was asleep in her recliner. That spell had really done a number on her. It was on my list of wrongs to right. But this one was top of the list. And I was glad she wasn't awake to talk me out of it.

I snuck out to the garage and made a circle with the salt.

Stevie stalked into the room. "Should I ask what you're doing?"

"Probably not," I said.

"You want to free another demon?"

"Not exactly," I said.

"I'll be in the shadow realm, just in case."

I downed the potion and summoned the demon Custos.

Only a few seconds passed before the circle began to fill

with black smoke. The demon slowly manifested again wearing his black suit and tie. While his face might've been beautiful once, eons of wickedness scored it like the face of an old man who worked in the sun his whole life.

"You... again?"

"Me... again," I said proudly.

The demon took in his surroundings, carefully measuring the circle and checking it for any hint of imperfection. There were none.

"You know," he said, "I can feel your power is weak. I might not be able to break the circle, but I could pull you in—I could take you back to my prison if I wanted."

"Something tells me you don't want to do that."

"No?" He raised a wicked eyebrow. "Why wouldn't I?"

"It would mean more work," I said. "Another soul to keep."

He looked around. There was no wine. No ice cream.

"I have something to barter," I told him.

"I don't want to barter," the demon snarled. "I want payment."

"Okay. Payment it is then."

"I'm listening."

"How long did you say Brad's sentence was?"

"A hundred years. Long enough you'll be out of the picture."

"Right." I nodded. "That's a long time."

"Not as long as an eternal life."

I stopped him.

"Time in the shadow realm doesn't mean much," I said. "But time here matters. Every second costs something."

"Is that a fact?"

"You're a prisoner in your own prison," I told him. "And

every second you get here in the real world, you cherish. I can see it on your face."

He smirked. "What are you getting at?"

"In a year and a day, I'll set you free. I won't call you into a binding circle. I'll let you go."

"Just like that?"

"For a limited time only," I said. "I'll let you out for one hour. That's the deal. That's the best I can do."

"You think you'll be able to stop me from extending my stay?" Why he didn't just take me up on the offer, I don't know. Instead, he'd used the moment to taunt me.

"Fine. Thirty minutes."

"But you—"

I clenched my fist, drawing as much power as I could, and tightened the circle around him. "I thought you were going to extend your stay. Why would thirty minutes less matter to you?"

He bared his fang-like teeth.

"Do we have a deal?" I asked.

"It's a deal," he growled. "Now, allow me to leave, and I'll return the familiar."

I let go of the magic in the circle, and he vanished in another puff of smoke. Before he was gone, he whispered, "You're not as clever as you think."

He probably had a point. I knew I wasn't being smart— the potion was making choices I'd have to answer for one day. Or in a year and one day. But that *did* give me some time to work through the problem.

My heart beat fast as I waited what felt like forever for Brad to appear in the circle. Not with a puff of smoke. He wasn't a demon. He finally materialized, bit by bit like he was beamed from the Enterprise.

And he wasn't a raccoon.

He was gorgeous. More angelic than the other fallen angels I'd seen. Even his wings were still feathered.

He wore a hardened expression on his face, no relief, nor a smile.

For the moment, my worries were gone. Everything I'd been through in the past so many weeks meant little.

Sure, I'd have to face that demon again. I'd have to send him back to his prison realm. But that was a battle for another day.

And my mom, wherever she was, I was going to find her. But not now.

Right now, Brad was it. I wanted to hug him. I could stay right here in this moment and just live. And be happy. But with that thought, a new emotion hit me.

*Fear.*

*Why isn't he smiling?*

Brad finally spoke. "Did you miss me?"

"That's the first thing you ask? We have time for that later."

"That's a funny word. And I've heard it twice in quite short order. Did you really promise my jailer time?"

"Yes." I stared down at the salt circle. Even though I was no longer willing magic into it, Brad couldn't get out of the circle. "Another thing we can talk about later."

He crossed his arms. "I assume you want a dog this time? Another cat for your Gran's collection?"

"I hadn't thought about it." I made to scuff out the circle.

He stopped me.

"Well, please do. The moment I step over, I should know."

"Really? You can't just stay like this?"

He shook his head.

"I can still read your thoughts," he said.

That wasn't a good thing. I stared into his coal black eyes for just a second too long. "I didn't miss you," I said honestly.

"Why not?"

"Because I hadn't gotten to know you. Because you were a raccoon and I didn't understand what familiars were for—what they could do."

"And now?"

"I know why I need you."

He squinted, and I knew he was reading my mind once more. His lips twisting into a smirk. "I don't believe it."

"It'll make things easier."

"For you or for me?"

"For both of us," I said.

He stepped across the circle.

And Brad, the raccoon, was home.

## 35

# CREEL CREEK AFTER DARK EPISODE 56

It's getting late.

Very late.

*The creeping dread of tomorrow haunts your dreams.*

*It's dark out. Are you afraid?*

*Welcome to Creel Creek After Dark.*

**Athena:** I'm your host, Athena Hunter.

**Ivana:** And I'm Ivana Steak.

**Athena:** Welcome to yet another episode of *Creel Creek After Dark*.

**Ivana:** Yet another, Athena? If I didn't know any better, I'd say you're sulking.

**Athena:** I'm not sulking. I'm upset. I'm *angry*.

**Ivana:** Can I just say that it's been a weird few weeks.

**Athena:** I guess so. You just said it.

**Ivana:** You're sure are sulking...

**Athena:** I was hexed last week. Let's not forget that. Definitive proof that witches *do* exist. And magic is real.

**Ivana:** To be fair, that's not exactly what your doctor says.

**Athena:** Hair loss brought on by sudden stress—does that sound plausible to you?

**Ivana:** Maybe that's the problem? It kinda does.

**Athena:** Whose side are you on?

**Ivana:** The listeners' side. We promised to only tell truths on this show.

**Athena:** And I'm telling the truth. I was hexed. And let's not forget what I found the other night in the woods.

**Ivana:** A jaw... I've seen it. It's gross.

**Athena:** Not just any jaw. We're sure. You know it's one of *theirs*. It's not human. And it's not from any animal native to our woods.

**Ivana:** So you've said...

**Athena:** It's proof, Ivana. *Definitive* proof.

**Ivana:** So you keep saying. Moving on... plans for the first annual Creel Creek Con—a convention celebrating all things after dark—are under way. Save the date for Halloween weekend and book your stay at the Creel Creek Mountain Lodge. Mention the show and get ten percent off of your stay.

**Ivana:** If you like witches, werewolves, or anything else that goes bump in the night, sign up for our newsletter. Tickets go on sale soon. And there will be a special signing event with yours truly. I might even bring misses surly along.

**Athena:** Ha... ha...

**Ivana:** See you soon. And sleep tight!

# EPILOGUE: IN WITCH I AM AT A LOSS FOR WORDS

It was a bright morning. The sun had already burned off Creel Creek's usual layer of fog.

I'd snuck away for a coffee at the new coffeeshop between Bewitched Books and the vape shop. It was a pleasant addition to a rather dismal strip of stores. They'd brought traffic in droves, and we'd even seen some spillover in the bookstore. Used books were being read again. *Finally.*

I was just turning the placard to open when my fingers tingled with witchy energy. There's no getting used to that—it's worse than getting shocked by a doorknob.

I peered into the dark recesses of the store and flipped on the lights. *Nothing amiss here*, I thought. But I knew better. I had to trust my witch instincts.

Outside, there were more cars than usual. And quite a few people on the sidewalk.

A woman with a toddler struggled with a car seat, leaving her coffee cup on the top of the car. She was just about to drive away, then remembered.

Her parking spot wasn't open long. A black Chevrolet Caprice Classic straight from an early Nineties police movie pulled in. The driver, a man in a dark coat with a dark hat and sunglasses, eyed me. I smiled at him and moved away from the door, expecting that he—like everyone else—was here for coffee.

But the door jingled a half second later, startling me all over again. Behind the counter, I jumped then tried to play it cool.

He sighed and tore off his glasses, breathing the shop in —the stale smell of old books. Then he came toward me, his eyes locked on mine.

My heart began to race.

*Who is this guy?*

"Hello, Constance Campbell." He rested his hands on the counter, smiling, and said, "My name is Ivan Rush. I work for an organization known as the Faction. I hear you've been looking for us..."

# CREEL CREEK AFTER DARK EPISODE 1

**Athena:** Testing. Testing. Is this thing on?

**Ivana:** It's on. Are you ready?

**Athena:** Yes.

**Ivana:** Great! Welcome to Creel Creek Confidential. The first all true podcast about the supernatural.

**Athena:** It's Creel Creek After Dark, remember?

**Ivana:** Oh, right. Right. I remember. Someone thinks Creel Creek After Dark is a better title.

**Athena:** Because it is. *I'm* that someone. And I'm your host, Athena Hunter. I'm also an expert negotiator.

**Ivana:** That you are, Athena. Which reminds me, I'm stuck in a rut. I've been working the same job for the same pay for far too long now. I need tutoring from an expert negotiator.

**Athena:** One day, Ivana, we're both going to spread our wings and fly. Much like some of the citizens here in Creel Creek. Maybe we should take a few minutes to explain what the podcast is about?

**Ivana:** A few minutes? Maybe we should use the rest of the episode?

**Athena:** Yes. An even better plan.

**Ivana:** I'm your cohost, Ivana Steak. And we're here in Virginia's spookiest town, Creel Creek, to uncover the hidden truths behind its folk tales and urban legends.

**Athena:** You know what I was just thinking?

**Ivana:** That you're going off script again?

**Athena:** Besides that. I was thinking we need some intro music. And some dark and sinister voice to segue into the show. I guess that's something to think about for next episode.

**Ivana:** If there *is* a next episode. I might quit if my cohost won't quit going off script.

**Athena:** Fair enough, Ivana. Fair enough…

*Creel Creek After Dark: The Lost Episodes,* a newsletter exclusive coming this summer. Sign up to the newsletter for that and more!

You can also find me on Facebook here: http://facebook.com/christinezanebooks

## ALSO BY CHRISTINE ZANE THOMAS

**Witching Hour starring 40 year old witch Constance Campbell**

Book 1: Midlife Curses

Book 2: Never Been Hexed

Book 3: Must Love Charms

Book 4: You've Got Spells

**Witching Hour: Psychics coming early 2021**

Book 1: The Scrying Game

**Tessa Randolph Cozy Mysteries written with Paula Lester**

Grim and Bear It

The Scythe's Secrets

Reap What She Sows

**Foodie File Mysteries starring Allie Treadwell**

The Salty Taste of Murder

A Choice Cocktail of Death

A Juicy Morsel of Jealousy

The Bitter Bite of Betrayal

**Comics and Coffee Case Files starring Kirby Jackson and Gambit**

Book 1: Marvels, Mochas, and Murder

Book 2: Lattes and Lies

Book 3: Cold Brew Catastrophe

Book 4: Decaf Deceit

This Book: Coffee Shop Capers

# ABOUT CHRISTINE ZANE THOMAS

Christine Zane Thomas is the pen name of a husband and wife team. A shared love of mystery and sleuths spurred the creation of their own mysterious writer alter-ego.

While not writing, they can be found in northwest Florida with their two children, their dachshund Queenie, and schnauzer Tinker Bell. When not at home, their love of food takes them all around the South. Sometimes they sprinkle in a trip to Disney World. Food and Wine is their favorite season.

# ACKNOWLEDGMENTS

Thanks to Ellen Campbell who edited this book. To Sara Johnson for proofreading. To Jason and Hillary for beta reads, helping to steer this book in the right direction. And as always to our family and friends who help support our writing pursuits.

Printed in Great Britain
by Amazon